D0268007

BOURNEMOUTH LIBRARIES
610172573 W

THE NEW GIRL FRIEND AND OTHER STORIES

Ruth Rendell

CHIVERS LARGE PRINT
BATH

British Library Cataloguing in Publication Data available

This Large Print edition published by Chivers Press, Bath, 2000.

Published by arrangement with Random House UK Limited.

U.K. Hardcover ISBN 0 7540 4095 X
U.K. Softcover ISBN 0 7540 4096 8

Photoset, printed and bound in Great Britain by
Redwood Books, Trowbridge, Wiltshire

For Paul Sidey

CONTENTS

The New Girl Friend	1
A Dark Blue Perfume	18
The Orchard Walls	34
Hare's House	57
Bribery and Corruption	74
The Whistler	92
The Convolvulus Clock	119
Loopy	139
Fen Hall	159
Father's Day	181
The Green Road to Quephanda	200

THE NEW GIRL FRIEND

'You know what we did last time?' he said.

She had waited for this for weeks. 'Yes?'

'I wondered if you'd like to do it again.'

She longed to but she didn't want to sound too keen. 'Why not?'

'How about Friday afternoon, then? I've got the day off and Angie always goes to her sister's on Friday.'

'Not *always*, David.' She giggled.

He also laughed a little. 'She will this week. Do you think we could use your car? Angie'll take ours.'

'Of course. I'll come for you about two, shall I?'

'I'll open the garage doors and you can drive straight in. Oh, and Chris, could you fix it to get back a bit later? I'd love it if we could have the whole evening together.'

'I'll try,' she said, and then, 'I'm sure I can fix it. I'll tell Graham I'm going out with my new girl friend.'

He said goodbye and that he would see her on Friday. Christine put the receiver back. She had almost given up expecting a call from him. But there must have been a grain of hope still, for she had never left the receiver off the way she used to.

The last time she had done that was on a Thursday three weeks before, the day she had gone round to Angie's and found David there alone. Christine had got into the habit of taking the phone off the hook during the middle part of the day to avoid getting calls for the Midland Bank. Her number and the Midland Bank's differed by only one digit. Most days she took the receiver off at nine-thirty and put it back at three-thirty. On Thursday afternoons she nearly always went round to see Angie and never bothered to phone first.

Christine knew Angie's husband quite well. If she stayed a bit later on Thursdays she saw him when he came home from work. Sometimes she and Graham and Angie and David went out together as a foursome. She knew that David, like Graham, was a salesman or sales executive, as Graham always described himself, and she guessed from her friend's life style that David was rather more successful at it. She had never found him particularly attractive, for, although he was quite tall, he had something of a girlish look and very fair wavy hair.

Graham was a heavily built, very dark man with a swarthy skin. He had to shave twice a day. Christine had started going out with him when she was fifteen and they had got married on her eighteenth birthday. She had never really known any other men at all intimately and now if she ever found herself alone with a man she felt awkward and apprehensive. The truth was that she was afraid a man might make an advance to her and the thought of that frightened her very much. For a long while she carried a penknife in her handbag in case she should need to defend herself. One evening, after they had been out with a colleague of Graham's and had had a few drinks, she told Graham about this fear of hers.

He said she was silly but he seemed rather pleased.

'When you went off to talk to those people and I was left with John I felt like that. I felt terribly nervous. I didn't know how to talk to him.'

Graham roared with laughter. 'You don't mean you thought old John was going to make a pass at you in the middle of a crowded restaurant?'

'I don't know,' Christine said. 'I never know what they'll do.'

'So long as you're not afraid of what I'll do,' said Graham, beginning to kiss her, 'that's all that matters.'

There was no point in telling him now, ten years too late, that she was afraid of what he did and always had been. Of course she had got used to it, she wasn't actually terrified, she was resigned and sometimes even quite cheerful about it. David was the only man she had ever been alone with when it felt all right.

That first time, that Thursday when Angie had gone to her sister's and hadn't been able to get through on the phone and tell Christine not to come, that time it had been fine. And afterwards she had felt happy and carefree, though what had happened with David took on the colouring of a dream next day. It wasn't really believable. Early on he had said:

'Will you tell Angie?'

'Not if you don't want me to.'

'I think it would upset her, Chris. It might even wreck our marriage. You see . . .' He had hesitated. 'You see, that was the first time I—I mean, anyone ever . . .' And he had looked into her eyes. 'Thank God it was you.'

The following Thursday she had gone round to see Angie as usual. In the meantime there had been no word from David. She stayed late in order to see him, beginning to feel a little sick with apprehension, her heart beating hard when he came in.

He looked quite different from how he had when she had found him sitting at the table reading, the radio on. He was wearing a grey flannel suit and a grey striped tie. When Angie went out of the room and for a minute she was alone with him, she felt a flicker of that old wariness that was the forerunner of her fear. He was getting her a drink. She looked up and met his eyes and it was all right again. He gave her a conspiratorial smile, laying a finger on his lips.

'I'll give you a ring,' he had whispered.

She had to wait two more weeks. During that time she went twice to Angie's and twice Angie came to her. She and Graham and Angie and David went out as a foursome and while Graham was fetching drinks and Angie was in the Ladies, David looked at her and smiled and lightly touched her foot with his foot under the table.

'I'll phonc you. I haven't forgotten.'

It was a Wednesday when he finally did phone. Next day Christine told Graham she had made a new friend, a girl she had met at work. She would be going out somewhere with this new friend on Friday and she wouldn't be back till eleven. She was desperately afraid he would want the car—it was *his* car or his firm's—but it so happened he would be in the office that day and would go by train. Telling him these lies didn't make her feel guilty. It wasn't as if this were some sordid affair, it was quite different.

When Friday came she dressed with great care. Normally, to go round to Angie's, she would have worn jeans and a tee shirt with a sweater over it. That was what she had on the first time she found herself alone with David. She put on a skirt and blouse and her black velvet jacket. She took the heated rollers out of her hair and brushed it into curls down on her shoulders. There was never much money to spend on clothes. The mortgage on the house took up a third of what Graham earned and half what she earned at her part-time job. But she could run to a pair of sheer black tights to go with the highest heeled shoes she'd got, her black pumps.

The doors of Angie and David's garage were wide open and their car was gone. Christine turned into their driveway, drove into the garage and closed the doors behind her. A door at the back of the garage led into the yard and garden. The kitchen door was unlocked as it had been that Thursday three weeks before and always was on Thursday afternoons. She opened the door and walked in.

'Is that you, Chris?'

The voice sounded very male. She needed to be reassured by the sight of him. She went into the hall as he came down the stairs.

'You look lovely,' he said.

'So do you.'

He was wearing a suit. It was of navy silk with a pattern of pink and white flowers. The skirt was very short, the jacket clinched into his waist with a wide navy patent belt. The long golden hair fell to his shoulders, he was heavily made-up and this time he had painted his fingernails. He looked far more beautiful than he had that first time.

* * *

Then, three weeks before, the sound of her entry drowned in loud music from the radio, she had come upon this girl sitting at the table reading *Vogue*. For a moment she had thought it must be David's sister. She had forgotten Angie had said David was an only child. The girl had long fair hair and was wearing a red summer dress with white spots on it, white sandals and around her neck a string of white beads. When Christine saw that it was not a girl but David himself she didn't know what to do.

He stared at her in silence and without moving and then he switched off the radio. Christine said the silliest and least relevant thing.

'What are you doing home at this time?'

That made him smile. 'I'd finished so I took the rest of the day off. I should have locked the back door. Now you're here you may as well sit down.'

She sat down. She couldn't take her eyes off him. He didn't look like a man dressed up as a girl, he looked like a girl and a much prettier one than she or Angie. 'Does Angie know?'

He shook his head.

'But why do you do it?' she burst out and she looked about the room, Angie's small, rather untidy living room, at the radio, the *Vogue* magazine. 'What do you get out of it?' Something came back to her from an article she had read. 'Did your mother dress you as a girl when you were little?'

'I don't know,' he said. 'Maybe. I don't remember. I don't want to *be* a girl. I just want to dress up as one sometimes.'

The first shock of it was past and she began to feel easier with him. It wasn't as if there was anything grotesque about the way he looked. The very last thing he reminded her of was one of those female impersonators. A curious thought came into her head, that it was *nicer*, somehow more civilized, to be a woman and that if only all men were more like women . . . That was silly, of course, it couldn't be.

'And it's enough for you just to dress up and be here on your own?'

He was silent for a moment. Then, 'Since you ask, what I'd really like would be to go out like this and . . .' He paused, looking at her, 'and be seen by lots of people, that's what I'd like. I've never had the nerve for that.'

The bold idea expressed itself without her having to give it a moment's thought. She wanted to do it. She was beginning to tremble with excitement.

'Let's go out then, you and I. Let's go out now. I'll put my car in your garage and you can get into it so the people next door don't see and then we'll go somewhere. Let's do that, David, shall we?'

She wondered afterwards why she had enjoyed it so much. What had it been, after all, as far as anyone else knew but two girls walking on Hampstead Heath? If Angie had suggested that the two of them do it she would have thought it a poor way of spending the afternoon. But with David... She hadn't even minded that of the two of them he was infinitely the better dressed, taller, better-looking, more graceful. She didn't mind now as he came down the stairs and stood in front of her.

'Where shall be go?'

'Not the Heath this time,' he said. 'Let's go shopping.'

He bought a blouse in one of the big stores. Christine went into the changing room with him when he tried it on. They walked about in Hyde Park. Later on they had dinner and Christine noted that they were the only two women in the restaurant dining together.

'I'm grateful to you,' David said. He put his hand over hers on the table.

'I enjoy it,' she said. 'It's so—crazy. I really love it. You'd better not do that, had you? There's a man over there giving us a funny look.'

'Women hold hands,' he said.

'Only *those* sort of women. David, we could do this every Friday you don't have to work.'

'Why not?' he said.

There was nothing to feel guilty about. She wasn't harming Angie and she wasn't being disloyal to Graham. All she was doing was going on innocent outings with another girl. Graham wasn't interested in her new friend, he didn't even ask her name. Christine came to long for Fridays, especially for the moment when she let herself into Angie's house and saw David coming down the stairs and for the moment when they stepped out of the car in some public place and the first eyes were turned on him. They went to Holland Park, they went to the zoo, to Kew Gardens. They went to the cinema and a man sitting next to David put his hand on his knee. David loved that, it was a triumph for him, but Christine whispered they must change their seats and they did.

When they parted at the end of an evening he kissed her gently on the lips. He smelled of Alliage or Je Reviens or Opium. During the afternoon they usually went into one of the big stores and sprayed themselves out of the tester bottles.

* * *

Angie's mother lived in the north of England. When she had to convalesce after an operation Angie went up there to look after her. She expected to be away two weeks and the second weekend of her absence Graham had to go to Brussels with the sales manager.

'We could go away somewhere for the weekend,' David said.

'Graham's sure to phone,' Christine said.

'One night then. Just for the Saturday night. You can tell him you're going out with your new girl friend and you're going to be late.'

'All right.'

It worried her that she had no nice clothes to wear. David had a small but exquisite wardrobe of suits and dresses, shoes and scarves and beautiful underclothes. He kept them in a cupboard in his office to which only he had a key and he secreted items home and back again in his briefcase. Christine hated the idea of going away for the night in her grey flannel skirt and white silk blouse and that velvet jacket while David wore his Zandra Rhodes dress. In a burst of recklessness she spent all of two weeks' wages on a linen suit.

They went in David's car. He had made the arrangements and Christine had expected they would be going to a motel twenty miles outside London. She hadn't thought it would matter much to David where they went. But he surprised her by his choice of an hotel that was a three-hundred-year-old house on the Suffolk coast.

'If we're going to do it,' he said, 'we may as well do it in style.'

She felt very comfortable with him, very happy. She tried to imagine what it would have felt like going to spend a night in an hotel with a man, a lover. If the person sitting next to her were dressed, not in a black and white printed silk dress and scarlet jacket but in a man's suit with shirt and tie. If the face it gave her so much pleasure to look at were not powdered and rouged and mascara'd but rough and already showing beard growth. She couldn't imagine it. Or, rather, she could only think how in that case she would have jumped out of the car at the first red traffic lights.

They had single rooms next door to each other. The rooms were very small but Christine could see that a double might have been awkward for David who must at some point—though she didn't care to think of this—have to shave and strip down to being what he really was.

He came in and sat on her bed while she unpacked her nightdress and spare pair of shoes.

'This is fun, isn't it?'

She nodded, squinting into the mirror, working on her eyelids with a little brush. David always did his eyes beautifully. She turned round and smiled at him.

'Let's go down and have a drink.'

The dining room, the bar, the lounge were all low-ceilinged timbered rooms with carved wood on the walls David said was called linenfold panelling. There were old maps and pictures of men hunting in gilt frames and copper bowls full of roses. Long windows were thrown open on to a terrace. The sun was still high in the sky and it was very warm. While Christine sat on the terrace in the sunshine David went off to get their drinks. When he came back to their table he had a man with him, a thickset paunchy man of about forty who was carrying a tray with four glasses on it.

'This is Ted,' David said.

'Delighted to meet you,' Ted said. 'I've asked my friend to join us. I hope you don't mind.'

She had to say she didn't. David looked at her and from his look she could tell he had deliberately picked Ted up.

'But why did you?' she said to him afterwards. 'Why did you want to? You told me you didn't really like it when that man put his hand on you in the cinema.'

'That was so physical. This is just a laugh. You don't suppose I'd let them touch me, do you?'

Ted and Peter had the next table to theirs at dinner. Christine was silent and standoffish but David flirted with them. Ted kept leaning across and whispering to him and David giggled and smiled. You could see he was enjoying himself tremendously. Christine knew they would ask her and David to go out with them after dinner and she began to be afraid. Suppose David got carried away by the excitement of it, the 'fun', and went off somewhere with Ted, leaving her and Peter alone together? Peter had a red face and black moustache and beard and a wart with black hairs growing out of it on his left cheek. She and David were eating steak and the waiter had brought them sharp pointed steak knives. She hadn't used hers. The steak was very tender. When no one was looking she slipped the steak knife into her bag.

Ted and Peter were still drinking coffee and brandies when David got up quite abruptly and said, 'Coming?' to Christine.

'I suppose you've arranged to meet them later?' Christine said as soon as they were out of the dining room.

David looked at her. His scarlet-painted lips parted into a wide smile. He laughed.

'I turned them down.'

'Did you *really*?'

'I could tell you hated the idea. Besides, we want to be alone, don't we? I know I want to be alone with you.'

She nearly shouted his name so that everyone could hear, the relief was so great. She controlled herself but she was trembling. 'Of course I want to be alone with you,' she said.

She put her arm in his. It wasn't uncommon, after all, for girls to walk along with linked arms. Men turned to look at David and one of them whistled. She knew it must be David the whistle was directed at because he looked so beautiful with his long golden hair and high-heeled red sandals. They walked along the sea front, along the little low promenade. It was too warm even at eight-thirty to wear a coat. There were a lot of people about but not crowds for the place was too select to attract crowds. They walked to the end of the pier. They had a drink in the Ship Inn and another in the Fishermen's Arms. A man tried to pick David up in the Fishermen's Arms but this time he was cold and distant.

'I'd like to put my arm round you,' he said as they were walking back, 'but I suppose that wouldn't do, though it is dark.'

'Better not,' said Christine. She said suddenly, 'This has been the best evening of my life.'

He looked at her. 'You really mean that?'

She nodded. 'Absolutely the best.'

They came into the hotel. 'I'm going to get them to send us up a couple of drinks. To my room. Is that OK?'

She sat on the bed. David went into the bathroom. To do his face, she thought, maybe to shave before he let the man with the drinks see him. There was a knock at the door and a waiter came in with a tray on which were two long glasses of something or other with fruit and leaves floating in it, two pink table napkins, two olives on sticks and two peppermint creams wrapped up in green paper.

Christine tasted one of the drinks. She ate an olive. She opened her handbag and took out a mirror and a lipstick and painted her lips. David came out of the bathroom. He had taken off the golden wig and washed his face. He hadn't shaved, there was a pale stubble showing on his chin and cheeks. His legs and feet were bare and he was wearing a very masculine robe made of navy blue towelling. She tried to hide her disappointment.

'You've changed,' she said brightly.

He shrugged. 'There are limits.'

He raised his glass and she raised her glass and he said: 'To us!'

The beginnings of a feeling of panic came over her. Suddenly he was so evidently a man. She edged a little way along the mattress.

'I wish we had the whole weekend.'

She nodded nervously. She was aware her body had started a faint trembling. He had noticed it too. Sometimes before he had noticed how emotion made her tremble.

'Chris,' he said.

She sat passive and afraid.

'I'm not really like a woman, Chris. I just play at that sometimes for fun. You know that, don't you?' The hand that touched her smelt of nail varnish remover. There were hairs on the wrist she had never noticed before. 'I'm falling in love with you,' he said. 'And you feel the same, don't you?'

She couldn't speak. He took her by the shoulders. He brought his mouth up to hers and put his arms round her and began kissing her. His skin felt abrasive and a smell as male as Graham's came off his body. She shook and shuddered. He pushed her down on the bed and his hands began undressing her, his mouth still on hers and his body heavy on top of her.

She felt behind her, put her hand into the open handbag and pulled out the knife. Because she could feel his heart beating steadily against her right breast she knew where to stab and she stabbed again and again. The bright red heart's blood spurted over her clothes and the bed and the two peppermint creams on the tray.

A DARK BLUE PERFUME

It would be true to say that not a day had passed without his thinking of her. Except for the middle years. There had been other women then to distract him, though no one he cared for enough to make his second wife. But once he was into his fifties the memory of her returned with all its old vividness. He would see other men settling down into middle age, looking towards old age, with loving wives beside them, and he would say to himself, Catherine, Catherine . . .

He had never, since she left him, worked and lived in his native land. He was employed by a company which sent him all over the world. For years he had lived in South America, Africa, the West Indies, coming home only on leave and not always then. He meant to come home when he retired, though, and to this end, on one of those leaves, he had bought himself a house. It was in the city where he and she had been born, but he had chosen a district as far as possible from the one in which she had gone to live with her new husband and a long way from where they had once lived together, for the time when he had bought it was the time when he had begun daily to think of her again.

He retired when he was sixty-five and came

home. He flew home and sent the possessions he had accumulated by sea. They included the gun he had acquired forty years before and with which he had intended to shoot himself when things became unendurable. But they had never been quite unendurable even then. Anger against her and hatred for her had sustained him and he had never got so far as even loading the small, unused automatic.

It was winter when he got home, bleak and wet and far colder than he remembered. When the snow came he stayed indoors, keeping warm, seeing no one. There was no one to see, anyway, they had gone away or died.

When his possessions arrived in three trunks—that was all he had amassed in forty years, three trunkfuls of bric-à-brac—he unpacked wonderingly. Only the gun had been put in by him, his servant had packed the rest. Things came to light he had long forgotten he owned, books, curios, and in an envelope he thought he had destroyed in those early days, all his photographs of her.

He sat looking at them one evening in early spring. The woman who came to clean for him had brought him a bowl of blue hyacinths and the air was heavy and languorous with the sweet scent of them. Catherine, Catherine, he said as he looked at the picture of her in their garden, the picture of her at the seaside, her hair blowing. How different his life would have been if she had stayed with him! If he had been a complaisant husband and borne it all and taken it all and forgiven her. But how could he have borne that? How could he have kept her when she was pregnant with another man's child?

The hyacinths made him feel almost faint. He pushed the photographs back into the envelope but he seemed to see her face still through the thick, opaque, brown paper. She had been a bit older than he, she would be nearly seventy now. She would be old, ugly, fat perhaps, arthritic perhaps, those firm cheeks fallen into jowls, those eyes sunk in folds of skin, that white column of a neck become a bundle of strings, that glossy chestnut hair a bush of grey. No man would want her now.

He got up and looked in the mirror over the mantelpiece. He hadn't aged much, hadn't changed much. Everyone said so. Of course it was true that he hadn't lived much, and it was living that aged you. He wasn't bald, he was thinner than he had been at twenty-five, his eyes were still bright and wistful and full of hope. Those four years' seniority she had over him, they would show now if they stood side by side.

She might be dead. He had heard nothing, there had been no news since the granting of the divorce and her marriage to that man. Aldred Sydney. Aldred Sydney might be dead, she might be a widow. He thought of what that name, in any context, had meant to him, how emotive it had been.

'I want you to meet the new general manager, Sydney Robinson.'

'Ycs, we're being sent to Australia, Sydney actually.'

'Cameron and Sydney, Surveyors and Valuers. Can I help you?'

For a long time he had trembled when he heard her surname pronounced. He had wondered how it could come so unconcernedly off another's tongue. Aldred Sydney would be no more than seventy, there was no reason to suppose him dead.

'Do you know Aldred and Catherine Sydney? They live at number 22. An elderly couple, yes, that's right. They're so devoted to each other, it's rather sweet . . .'

She wouldn't still live there, not after forty years. He went into the hall and fetched the telephone directory. For a moment or two he sat still, the book lying in his lap, breathing deeply because his heart was beating so fast. Then he opened the directory and turned to the S's. Aldred was such an uncommon name, there was probably only one Aldred Sydney in the country. He couldn't find him there, though there were many A. Sydneys living at addresses which had no meaning for him, no significance. He wondered afterwards why he had bothered to look lower, to let his eyes travel down through the B's and find her name, unmistakably, incontrovertibly, hers. Sydney, Catherine, 22 Aurora Road . . .

She was still there, she still lived there, and the phone was in her name. Aldred Sydney must be dead. He wished he hadn't looked in the phone book. Why had he? He could hardly sleep at all that night and when he awoke from a doze early in the morning, it was with her name on his lips: Catherine, Catherine.

He imagined phoning her.

'Catherine?'

'Yes, speaking. Who's that?'

'Don't you know? Guess. It's a long long time ago, Catherine.'

It was possible in fantasy, not in fact. He wouldn't know her voice now, if he met her in the street he wouldn't know her. At ten o'clock he got his car out and drove northwards, across the river and up through the northern suburbs. Forty years ago the place where she lived had been well outside the great metropolis, separated from it by fields and woods.

He drove through new streets, whole new districts. Without his new map he would have had no idea where he was. The countryside had been pushed away in those four decades. It hovered shyly on the outskirts of the little town that had become a suburb. And here was Aurora Road. He had never been to it before, never seen her house, though on any map he was aware of precisely where the street was, as if its name were printed in red to burn his eyes.

The sight of it at last, actually being there and seeing the house, made his head swim. He closed his eyes and sat there with his head bent over the wheel. Then he turned and looked at the neat, small house. Its paint was new and smart and the fifty-year-old front door had been replaced by a panelled oak one and the square bay by a bow window. But it was a poor, poky housc for all that. He sneered a little at dead Aldred Sydney who had done no better than this for his wife.

Suppose he were to go up to the door and ring the bell? But he wouldn't do that, the shock would be too much for her. He, after all, had prepared himself. She had no preparation for confronting that husband, so little changed, of long ago. Once, how he would have savoured the cruelty of it, the revenge! The handsome man, still looking middle aged, a tropical tan on his cheeks, his body flat and straight, and the broken old woman, squat now, grey, withered. He sighed. All desire for a cruel vengeance had left him. He wanted instead to be merciful, to be kind. Wouldn't the kindest thing be to leave her in peace? Leave her to her little house and the simple pursuits of old age.

He started the car again and drove a little way. It surprised him to find that Aurora Road was right on the edge of that retreating countryside, that its tarmac and grey paving stones led into fields. When she was younger she had possibly walked there sometimes, under the trees, along that footpath. He got out of the car and walked along it himself. After a time he saw a train in the distance, appearing and disappearing between green meadows, clumps of trees, clusters of red roofs, and then he came upon a signpost pointing to the railway station. Perhaps she had walked here to meet Aldred Sydney after his day's work.

He sat down on a rustic seat that had been placed at the edge of the path. It was a very pretty place, not spoilt at all, you could hardly see a single house. The grass was a pure, clean green, the hedgerows shimmering white with the tiny flowers of wild plum blossom which had a drier, sharper scent than the hyacinths. For the time of year it was warm and the sun was shining. A bumble bee, relict of the past summer, drifted by. He put his head back on the wooden bar of the seat and fell asleep.

It was an unpleasant dream he had, of those young days of his when he had been little more than a boy but she very much a grown woman. She came to him, as she had come then, and told him baldly, without shame or diffidence, that the child she carried wasn't his. In the dream she laughed at him, though he couldn't remember that she had done that in life, surely not. He jerked awake and for a moment he didn't know where he was. People talking, walking along the path, had roused him. He left the seat and the path and drove home.

All that week he meant to phone her. He longed fiercely to meet her. It was as if he were in love again, so full was he of obsessional yearnings and unsuspected fears and strange whims. One afternoon he told himself he would phone her at exactly four, when it got to four he would count ten and dial her number. But when four came and he had counted ten his arm refused to function and lift the receiver, it was as if his arm were paralyzed. What was the matter with him that he couldn't make a phone call to an old woman he had once known?

The next day he drove back to Aurora Road in the late afternoon. There were three elderly women walking along, walking abreast, but not going in the direction of her house, coming away from it. Was one of them she?

In the three faces, one pale and lined, one red and firm, the third waxen, sagging, he looked for the features of his Catherine. He looked for some vestige of her step in the way each walked. One of the women wore a burgundy-coloured coat, and pulled down over her grey hair, a burgundy felt hat, a shapeless pudding of a hat. Catherine had been fond of wine-red. She had worn it to be married in, married to him and perhaps also to Aldred Sydney. But this woman wasn't she, for as they passed him she turned and peered into the car and her eyes met his without a sign of recognition.

After a little while he drove down the street and, leaving the car, walked along the footpath. The petals of the plum blossom lay scattered on the grass and the may was coming into green bud. The sun shone faintly from a white, curdy sky. This time he didn't sit down on the seat but left the path to walk under the trees, for today the grass was dry and springy. In the distance he heard a train.

He was unprepared for so many people coming this way from the station. There must have been a dozen pass in the space of two minutes. He pretended to be walking purposefully, walking for his health perhaps, for what would they think he was doing, there under the trees without a companion, a sketching block or even a dog? The last went by—or he supposed it was the last. And then he heard soft footfalls, the sound light shoes make on a dry, sandy floor.

Afterwards he was to tell himself that he knew her tread. At the time, honestly, he wasn't quite sure, he didn't dare be, he couldn't trust his own memory. And when she appeared it was quite suddenly from where the path emerged from a tunnel of trees. She was walking towards Aurora Road and as she passed she was no more than ten yards from him.

He stood perfectly still, frozen and dumb. He felt that if he moved he might fall down dead.

She didn't walk fast but lightly and springily as she had always done, and the years lay on her as lightly and gently as those footfalls of hers lay on the sand. Her hair was grey and her slenderness a little thickened. There was a hint of a double chin and a faint coarsening of those delicate features—but no more than that. If he had remained young, so had she. It was as if youth had been preserved in each of them for this moment.

He wanted to see her eyes, the blue of those hyacinths, but she kept them fixed straight ahead of her, and she had quickly gone out of his sight, lost round a curve in the path. He crept to the seat and sat down. The wonder of it, the astonishment! He had imagined her old and found her young, but she had always surprised him. Her variety, her capacity to astound, were infinite.

She had come off the train with the others. Did she go out to work? At her age? Many did. Why not she? Sydney was dead and had left her, no doubt, ill-provided for. Sydney was dead... He thought of courting her again, loving her, forgiving her, wooing her.

'Will you marry me, Catherine?'

'Do you still want me—after everything?'

'Everything was only a rather long bad dream...'

She would come and live in his house and sit opposite him in the evenings, she would go on holiday with him, she would be his wife. They would have little jokes for their friends.

'How long have you two been married?'

'It was our second wedding anniversary last week and it will be our forty-fifth next month.'

He wouldn't phone, though. He would sit on this seat at the same time tomorrow and wait for her to pass by and recognize him.

Before he left home he studied the old photographs of himself that were with the old photographs of her. He had been fuller in the face then and he hadn't worn glasses. He put his hand to his high, sloping forehead and wondered why it looked so low in the pictures. Men's fashions didn't change much. The sports jacket he had on today was much like the sports jacket he had worn on his honeymoon.

As he was leaving the house he was assailed by the scent of the hyacinths, past their prime now and giving off a sickly, cloying odour. Dark blue flowers with a dark blue perfume... On an impulse he snapped off their heads and threw them into the wastepaper basket.

The day was bright and he slid back the sunshine roof on his car. When he got to Aurora Road, the field and the footpath, he took off his glasses and slipped them into his pocket. He couldn't see very well without them and he stumbled a little as he walked along.

There was no one on the seat. He sat down in the centre of it. He heard the train. Then he saw it, rattling along between the tufty trees and the little choppy red roofs and the squares of green. It was bringing him, he thought, his whole life's happiness. Suppose she didn't always catch that train, though? Or suppose yesterday's appearance had been an isolated happening, not a return from work but from some occasional visit?

He had hardly time to think about it before the commuters began to come, one and one and then two together. It looked as if there wouldn't be as many as there had been yesterday. He waited, holding his hands clasped together, and when she came he scarcely heard her, she walked so softly.

His sight was so poor without his glasses that she appeared to him as in a haze, almost like a spirit woman, a ghost. But it was she, her vigorous movements, her strong athletic walk, unchanged from her girlhood, and unchanged too, the atmosphere of her that he would have known if he had been not short-sighted but totally blind and deaf too.

The trembling which had come upon him again ceased as she approached and he fixed his eyes on her, half-rising from the seat. And now she looked at him also. She was very near and her face flashed suddenly into focus, a face on which he saw blankness, wariness, then slight alarm. But he was sure she recognized him. He tried to speak and his voice croaked out:

'Don't you know me?'

She began walking fast away, she broke into a run. Disbelieving, he stared after her. There was someone else coming along from the station now, a man who walked out of the tree tunnel and caught her up. They both looked back, whispering. It was then that he heard her voice, only a little older, a little harsher, than when they had first met. He got off the seat and walked about among the trees, holding his head in his hands. She had looked at him, she had seemed to know him—and then she hadn't wished to.

When he reached home again he understood what he had never quite faced up to when he first retired, that he had nothing to live for. For the past week he had lived for her and in the hope of having her again. He found his gun, the small unused automatic, and loaded it and put on the safety catch and looked at it. He would write to her and tell her what he had done—by the time she got his letter he would have done it—or, better still, he would see her once, force her to see him, and then he would do it.

The next afternoon he drove to her house in Aurora Road. It was nearly half-past five, she would be along at any moment. He sat in the car, feeling the hard bulge of the gun in his pocket. Presently the man who had caught her up the day before came along, but now he was alone, walking the length of Aurora Road and turning down a side street.

She was late. He left the car where it was and set off to find her, for he could no longer bear to sit there, the pain of it, the sick suspense. He kept seeing her face as she had looked at him, with distaste and then with fear.

Another train was jogging between the tree tufts and the little red chevrons, he heard it enter the station. Had the green, the many, varied greens, been as bright as this yesterday? The green of the grass and the new beech leaves and the may buds hurt his eyes. He passed the seat and went on, further than he had ever been before, coming into a darkish grove where the trees arched over the path. Her feet on the sand whispered like doves. He stood still, he waited for her.

She slowed down when she saw him and came on hesitantly, raising one hand to her face. He took a step towards her, saying, 'Please. Please don't go. I want to talk to you so much . . .'

Today he was wearing his glasses, there was no chance of his eyes being deceived. He couldn't be mistaken as to the meaning of her expression. It was compounded of hatred and terror. But this time she couldn't walk on without walking into his arms. She turned to hasten back the way she had come, and as she turned he shot her.

With the first shot he brought her down. He ran up to where she had fallen but he couldn't look at her, he could only see her as very small and very distant through a red haze of revenge. He shot her again and again, and at last the white ringless hand which had come feebly up to shield her face, fell in death.

The gun was empty. There was blood on him that had flown from her. He didn't care about that, he didn't care who saw or knew, so long as he could get home and re-load the gun for himself. It surprised him that he could walk, but he could and quite normally as far as he could tell. He was without feeling now, without pain or fear, and his breathing settled, though his heart still jumped. He gave the body on the ground one last vague look and walked away from it, out of the tree tunnel, on to the path. The sun made bright sheets of light on the grass and long, tapering shadows. He walked along Aurora Road towards the car outside her house.

Her front door opened as he was unlocking the car. An old woman came out. He recognized her as one of those he had seen on his second visit, the one who had been wearing the dark red coat and hat. She came to the gate and looked over it, looked up towards the left a little anxiously, then backed and smiled at him. Something in his state must have made her speak, show politeness to this stranger.

'I was looking for my daughter,' she said. 'She's a bit late today, she's usually on that first train.'

He put his cold hands on the bar of the gate. Her smile faded.

'Catherine,' he said, 'Catherine . . .'

She lifted to him enquiring eyes, blue as the hyacinths he had thrown away.

THE ORCHARD WALLS

I have never told anyone about this before.

The worst was long over, of course. Intense shame had faded and the knowledge of having made the greatest possible fool of myself. Forty years and more had done their work there. The feeling I had been left with, that I was precocious in a foul and dirty way, that I was unclean, was washed away. I had done my best never to think about it, to blot it all out, never to permit to ring on my inward ear Mrs Thorn's words:

'How dare you say such a thing! How dare you be so disgusting! At your age, a child, you must be sick in your mind.'

Things would bring it back, the scent of honeysuckle, a brace of bloodied pigeons hanging in a butcher's window, the first cherries of the season. I winced at these things, I grew hot with a shadow of that blush that had set me on fire with shame under the tree, Daniel's hard hand gripping my shoulder, Mrs Thorn trembling with indignant rage. The memory, never completely exorcised, still had the power to punish the adult for the child's mistake.

Until today.

Having one's childhood trauma cured by an analyst must be like this, only a newspaper has cured mine. The newspaper came through my door and told me I hadn't been disgusting or sick in my mind, I had been right. In the broad facts at least I had been right. All day I have been asking myself what I should do, what action, if any, I should take. At last I have been able to think about it all quite calmly, in tranquillity, to think of Ella and Dennis Clifton without growing hot and ashamed, of Mrs Thorn with pity and of that lovely lost place with something like nostalgia.

It was a long time ago. I was fourteen. Is that to be a child? They thought so, I thought so myself at the time. But the truth was I was a child and not a child, at one and the same time a paddler in streams, a climber of trees, an expert at cartwheels—and with an imagination full of romantic love. I was in a stage of transition, a pupa, a chrysalis, I was fourteen.

Bombs were falling on London. I had already once been evacuated with my school and come back again to the suburb we lived in that sometimes seemed safe and sometimes not. My parents were afraid for me and that was why they sent me to Inchfield, to the Thorns. I could see the fear in my mother's eyes and it made me uncomfortable.

'Just till the end of August,' she said, pleading with me. 'It's beautiful there. You could think of it as an extra long summer holiday.'

I remembered Hereford and my previous 'billet', the strange people, the alien food.

'This will be different. Ella is your own aunt.'

She was my mother's sister, her junior by twelve years. There were a brother and sister in between, both living in the north. Ella's husband was a farmer in Suffolk, or had been. He was in the army and his elder brother ran the farm. Later, when Ella was dead and Philip Thorn married again and all I kept of them was that shameful thing I did my best to forget, I discovered that Ella had married Philip when she was seventeen because she was pregnant and in the thirties any alternative to marriage in those circumstances was unthinkable. She had married him and six months later given birth to a dead child. When I went to Inchfield she was still only twenty-five, still childless, living with a brother-in-law and a mother-in-law in the depths of the country, her husband away fighting in North Africa.

I didn't want to go. At fourteen one isn't afraid, one knows one is immortal. After an air raid we used to go about the streets collecting pieces of shrapnel, fragments of shell. The worst thing to me was having to sleep under a Morrison shelter instead of in my bedroom. Having a room of my own again, a place to be private in, was an inducement. I yielded. To this day I don't know if I was invited or if my mother had simply written to say I was coming, that I must come, that they must give me refuge.

It was the second week of June when I went. Daniel Thorn met me at the station at Ipswich. I was wildly romantic, far too romantic, my head full of fantasies and dreams. Knowing I should be met, I expected a pony carriage or even a man on a black stallion leading a chestnut mare for me, though I had never in my life been on a horse. He came in an old Ford van.

We drove to Inchfield through deep green silent lanes—silent, that is, but for the occasional sound of a shot. I thought it must be something to do with the war, without specifying to myself what.

'The war?' said Daniel as if this were something happening ten thousand miles away. He laughed the age-old laugh of the countryman scoring off the townie. 'You'll find no war here. That's some chap out after rabbits.'

Rabbit was what we were to live on, stewed, roasted, in pies, relieved by wood pigeon. It was a change from London sausages but I have never eaten rabbit since, not once. The characteristic smell of it cooking, experienced once in a friend's kitchen, brought me violent nausea. What a devil's menu that would have been for me, stewed rabbit and cherry pie!

* * *

The first sight of the farm enchanted me. The place where I lived in Hereford had been a late-Victorian brick cottage, red and raw and ugly as poverty. I had scarcely seen a house like Cherry Tree Farm except on a calendar. It was long and low and thatched and its two great barns were thatched too. The low green hills and the dark clustering woods hung behind it. And scattered all over the wide slopes of grass were the cherry trees, one so close up to the house as to rub its branches against a window pane.

They came out of the front door to meet us, Ella and Mrs Thorn, and Ella gave me a white, rather cold, cheek to kiss. She didn't smile. She looked bored. It was better therefore than I had expected and worse. Ella was worse and Mrs Thorn was better. The place was ten times better, tea was like something I hadn't had since before the war, my bedroom was not only nicer than the Morrison shelter, it was nicer than my bedroom at home. Mrs Thorn took me up there when we had eaten the scones and currant bread and walnut cake.

It was low-ceilinged with the stone-coloured studs showing through the plaster. A patchwork quilt was on the bed and the walls were hung with a paper patterned all over with bunches of cherries. I looked out of the window.

'You can't see the cherry trees from here,' I said. 'Is that why they put cherries on the walls?'

The idea seemed to puzzle her. She was a simple conservative woman. 'I don't know about that. That would be rather whimsical.'

I was at the back of the house. My window overlooked a trim dull garden of rosebeds cut out in segments of a circle. Mrs Thorn's own garden, I was later to learn, and tended by herself.

'Who sleeps in the room with the cherry tree?' I said.

'Your auntie.' Mrs Thorn was always to refer to Ella in this way. She was a stickler for respect. 'That has always been my son Philip's room.'

Always . . . I envied the absent soldier. A tree with branches against one's bedroom window represented to me something down which one could climb and make one's escape, perhaps even without the aid of knotted sheets. I said as much, toning it down for my companion who I guessed would see it in a different light.

'I'm sure he did no such thing,' said Mrs. Thorn. 'He wasn't that kind of boy.'

Those words stamped Philip for me as dull. I wondered why Ella had married him. What had she seen in this unromantic chap, five years her senior, who hadn't been the kind of boy to climb down the trees out of his bedroom window? Or climb up them, come to that . . .

She was beautiful. For the first Christmas of the war I had been given *Picturegoer Annual* in which was a full-page photograph of Hedy Lamarr. Ella looked just like her. She had the same perfect features, dark hair, other-worldly eyes fixed on far horizons. I can see her now—I can *permit* myself to see her—as she was then, thin, long-legged, in the floral cotton dress with collar and cuffs and narrow belt that would be fashionable again today. Her hair was pinned up in a roll off her forehead, the rest left hanging to her shoulders in loose curls, mouth painted like raspberry jam, eyes as nature made them, large, dark, alight with some emotion I was years from analysing. I think now it was compounded of rebellion and longing and desire.

Sometimes in the early evenings she would disappear upstairs and then Mrs Thorn would say in a respectful voice that she had gone to write to Philip. We used to listen to the wireless. Of course no one knew exactly where Philip was but we all had a good idea he was somehow involved in the attempts to relieve Tobruk. At news times Mrs Thorn became very tense. Once, to my embarrassment, she made a choking sound and left the room, covering her eyes with her hand. Ella switched off the set.

'You ought to be in bed,' she said to me. 'When I was your age I was always in bed by eight.'

I envied and admired her, even though she was never particularly nice to me and seldom spoke except to say I 'ought' to be doing something or other. Did she look at this niece, not much more than ten years younger than herself, and see what she herself had thrown away, a future of hope, a chance of living?

I spent very little time with her. It was Mrs Thorn who took me shopping with her to Ipswich, who talked to me while she did the baking, who knitted and taught me to knit. There was no wool to be had so we unpicked old jumpers and washed the wool and carded it and started again. I was with her most of the time. It was either that or being on my own. No doubt there were children of my own age in the village I might have got to know but the village was two miles away. I was allowed to go out for walks but not to ride the only bicycle they had.

'It's too large for you, it's a twenty-eight inch,' Mrs Thorn said. 'Besides, it's got a crossbar.'

I said I could easily swing my leg behind the saddle like a man.

'Not while you're staying with me.'

I didn't understand. 'I wouldn't hurt myself.' I said what I said to my mother. 'I wouldn't come to any harm.'

'It isn't ladylike,' said Mrs Thorn, and that was that.

Those things mattered a lot to her. She stopped me turning cartwheels on the lawn when Daniel was about, even though I wore shorts. Then she made me wear a skirt. But she was kind, she paid me a lot of attention. If I had had to depend on Ella or the occasional word from Daniel I might have looked forward more eagerly to my parents' fortnightly visits than I did.

After I had been there two or three weeks the cherries began to turn colour. Daniel, coming upon me looking at them, said they were an old variety called Inchfield White Heart.

'There used to be a cherry festival here,' he said. 'The first Sunday after July the twelfth it was. There'd be dancing and a supper, you'd have enjoyed yourself. Still, we never had one last year and we're not this and somehow I don't reckon there'll ever be a cherry festival again what with this old war.'

He was a yellow-haired, red-complexioned Suffolk man, big and thickset. His wide mouth, sickle-shaped, had its corners permanently turned upwards. It wasn't a smile though and he was seldom cheerful. I never heard him laugh. He used to watch people in rather a disconcerting way, Ella especially. And when guests came to the house, Dennis Clifton or Mrs Leithman or some of the farming people they knew, he would sit and watch them, seldom contributing a word.

One evening, when I was coming back from a walk, I saw Ella and Dennis Clifton kissing in the wood.

* * *

Dennis Clifton wasn't a farmer. He had been in the R.A.F., had been a fighter pilot in the Battle of Britain but had received some sort of head injury, been in hospital and was now on leave at home recuperating. He must have been very young, no more than twenty-two or three. While he was ill his mother, with whom he had lived and who had been a friend of Mrs Thorn's, had died and left him her pretty little Georgian house in Inchfield. He was often at the farm, ostensibly to see his mother's old friend.

After these visits Daniel used to say, 'He'll soon be back in the thick of it,' or 'It won't be long before he's up there in his Spitfire. He can't wait.'

This made me watch him too, looking for signs of impatience to return to the R.A.F. His hands shook sometimes, they trembled like an old man's. He too was fair-haired and blue-eyed, yet there was all the difference in the world between his appearance and Daniel's. Film stars set my standard of beauty and I thought he looked like Leslie Howard playing Ashley Wilkes. He was tall and thin and sensitive and his eyes were sad. Daniel watched him and Ella sat silent and I read my book while he talked very kindly and encouragingly to Mrs Thorn about her son Philip, about how confident he was Philip would be all right, would survive, and while he talked his eyes grew sadder and more veiled.

No, I have imagined that, not remembered it. It is in the light of what I came to know that I have imagined it. He was simply considerate and kind like the well-brought-up young man he was.

I had been in the river. There was a place about a mile upstream they called the weir where for a few yards the banks were built up with concrete below a shallow fall. A pool about four feet deep had formed there and on hot days I went bathing in it. Mrs. Thorn would have stopped me if she had known but she didn't know. She didn't even know I had a bathing costume with me.

The shortest way back was through the wood. I heard a shot and then another from up in the meadows. Daniel was out after pigeons. The wood was dim and cool, full of soft twitterings, feathers rustling against dry leaves. The bluebells were long past but dog's mercury was in flower, a white powdering, and the air was scented with honeysuckle. Another shot came, further off but enough to shatter peace, and there was a rush of wings as pigeons took flight. Through the black trunks of trees and the lacework of their branches I could see the yellow sky and the sun burning in it, still an hour off setting.

Ella was leaning against the trunk of a

chestnut, looking up into Dennis Clifton's face. He had his hands pressed against the trunk, on either side of her head. If she had ever been nice to me, if he had ever said more than hallo, I think I might have called out to them. I didn't call and in a moment I realized the last thing they would want was to be seen.

I stayed where I was. I watched them. Oh, I was in no way a voyeur. There was nothing lubricious in it, nothing of curiosity, still less a wish to catch them out. I was overwhelmed rather by the romance of it, ravished by wonder. I watched him kiss her. He took his hands down and put his arms round her and kissed her so that their faces were no longer visible, only his fair head and her dark hair and their locked straining shoulders. I caught my breath and shivered in the warm half-light, in the honeysuckle air.

They left the place before I did, walking slowly away in the direction of the road, arms about each other's waists. In the room at Cherry Tree Farm they still called the parlour Mrs Thorn and Daniel were sitting, listening to the wireless, drinking tea. No more than five minutes afterwards Ella came in. I had seen what I had seen but if I hadn't, wouldn't I still have thought her looks extraordinary, her shining eyes and the flush on her white cheeks, the willow leaf in her hair and the bramble clinging to her skirt?

Daniel looked at her. There was blood in his fingernails, though he had scrubbed his hands. It brought me a flicker of nausea. Ella put her fingers through her hair, plucked out the leaf and went upstairs.

'She is going up to write to Philip,' said Mrs Thorn.

Why wasn't I shocked? Why wasn't I horrified? I was only fourteen and I came from a conventional background. Adultery was something committed by people in the Bible. I suppose I could say I had seen no more than a kiss and adultery didn't enter into it. Yet I knew it did. With no experience, with only the scantiest knowledge, I sensed that this love had its full consummation. I knew Ella was married to a soldier who was away fighting for his country. I even knew that my parents would think behaviour such as hers despicable if not downright wicked. But I cared for none of that. To me it was romance, it was Lancelot and Guinevere, it was a splendid and beautiful adventure that was happening to two handsome young people—as one day it might happen to me.

* * *

I was no go-between. For them I scarcely existed. I received no words or smiles, still less messages to be carried. They had the phone, anyway, they had cars. But though I took no part in their love affair and wasn't even with accuracy able to calculate the times when it was conducted, it filled my thoughts. Outwardly I followed the routine of days I had arranged for myself and Mrs Thorn had arranged for me, but my mind was occupied with Dennis and Ella, assessing what meeting places they would use, imagining their conversations—their vows of undying love—and re-creating with cinematic variations that kiss.

My greatest enjoyment, my finest hours of empathy, were when he called. I watched the two of them as intently then as Daniel did. Sometimes I fancied I caught between them a glance of longing and once I actually witnessed something more, an encounter between them in the passage when Ella came from the kitchen with the tea tray and Dennis had gone to fetch something from his car for Mrs Thorn. Unseen by them, I stood in the shadow between the grandfather clock and the foot of the stairs. I heard him whisper.

'Tonight? Same place?'

She nodded, her eyes wide. I saw him put his hand on her shoulder in a slow caress as he went past her.

I slept badly those nights. It had become very hot. Mrs Thorn made sure I was in bed by nine and there was no way of escaping from the house after that without being seen by her. I envied

Ella with a tree outside her window down which it would be easy to climb and escape. I imagined going down to the river in the moonlight, walking in the wood, perhaps seeing my lovers in some trysting place. My lovers, whose breathy words and laden glances exalted me and rarefied the overheated air . . .

The cherries were turning pale yellow with a blush coming to their cheeks. It was the first week of July, the week the war came to Inchfield and a German bomber, lost and off course, unloaded a stick of bombs in one of the Thorns' fields.

No one was hurt, though a cow got killed. We went to look at the mess in the meadow, the crater and the uprooted tree. Daniel shook his fist at the sky. The explosions had made a tremendous noise and we were all sensitive after that to any sudden sound. Even the crack of Daniel's shotgun made his mother jump.

The heat had turned sultry and clouds obscured out blue skies, though no rain fell. Mrs Leithman, coming to tea as she usually did once in the week, told us she fancied each roll of thunder was another bomb. We hardly saw Ella, she was always up in her room or out somewhere—out with Dennis, of course. I speculated about them, wove fantasies around them, imagined Philip Thorn killed in battle and thereby setting them free. So innocent was I, living in more innocent or at least more puritanical times, that the possibility of this childless couple being divorced never struck me. Nor did I envisage Dennis and Ella married to each other but only continuing for ever their perilous enchanting idyll. I even found Juliet's lines for them—Juliet who was my own age—and whispered to myself that the orchard walls are high and hard to climb and the place death, considering who thou art . . . Once, late at night when I couldn't sleep and sat in my window, I saw the shadowy figure of Dennis Clifton emerge from the deep darkness at the side of the house and leave by the gate out of the rose garden.

But the destruction of it all and my humiliation were drawing nearer. I had settled down there, I had begun to be happy. The truth is, I suppose, that I identified with Ella and in my complex fantasies it was I, compounded with Juliet, that Dennis met and embraced and touched and loved. My involvement was much deeper than that of an observer.

When it came the shot sounded very near. It woke me up as such a sound might not have done before the bombs. I wondered what prey Daniel could go in search of at this hour, for the darkness was deep, velvety and still. The crack which had split the night and jarred the silence wasn't repeated. I went back to sleep and slept till past dawn.

I got up early as I did most mornings, came

downstairs in the quiet of the house, the hush of a fine summer morning, and went outdoors. Mrs Thorn was in the kitchen, frying fat bacon and duck eggs for the men. I didn't know if it was all right for me to do this or if all the cherries were reserved for some mysterious purpose, but as I went towards the gate I reached up and picked a ripe one from a dipping branch. It was the crispest sweetest cherry I have ever tasted, though I must admit I have eaten few since then. I pushed the stone into the earth just inside the gates. Perhaps it germinated and grew. Perhaps quite an old tree that has borne many summer loads of fruit now stands at the entrance to Cherry Tree Farm.

As it happened, of all their big harvest, that was the only cherry I was ever to eat there. Coming back half an hour later, I pushed open the gate and stood for a moment looking at the farmhouse over whose sunny walls and roof the shadows of the trees lay in a slanted leafy pattern. I looked at the big tree, laden with red-gold fruit, that rubbed its branches against Ella's window. In its boughs, halfway up, in a fork a yard or two from the glass, hung the body of a man.

★ ★ ★

In the hot sunshine I felt icy cold. I remember the feeling to this day, the sensation of being frozen by a cold that came from within while outside me the sun shone and a thrush sang and the swallows dipped in and out under the eaves. My eyes seemed fixed, staring in the hypnosis of shock and fear at the fair-haired dangling man, his head thrown back in the agony of death there outside Ella's bedroom window.

At least I wasn't hysterical. I resolved I must be calm and adult. My teeth were chattering. I walked stiffly into the kitchen and there they all were, round the table, Daniel and the two men and Ella and, at the head of it, Mrs Thorn pouring tea.

I meant to go quietly up to her and whisper it. I couldn't. To get myself there without running, stumbling, shouting, had used up all the control I had. The words rushed out in a loud ragged bray and I remember holding up my hands, my fists clenched.

'Mr Clifton's been shot. He's been shot, he's dead. His body's in the cherry tree outside Ella's window!'

There was silence. But first a clatter as of knives and forks dropped, of cups rattled into saucers, of chairs scraped. Then this utter stricken silence. I have never—not in all the years since then—seen anyone go as white as Ella went. She was as white as paper and her eyes were black holes. A brick colour suffused Daniel's face. He swore. He used words that made me shrink and draw back and shiver and stare from one to the other of the horrible, horrified faces.

Mrs Thorn was the first to speak, her voice cold with anger.

'How dare you say such a thing! How dare you be so disgusting! At your age—you must be sick in your mind.'

Daniel had jumped up. He took me roughly by the arm. But his grasp wasn't firm, the hand was shaking the way Dennis's shook. He manhandled me out there, his mother scuttling behind us. We were still five or six yards from the tree when I saw. The hot blood came into my face and throbbed under my skin. I looked at the cloth face, the yellow wool hair—our own unpicked carded wool—the stuffed sacking body, the cracked boots . . .

Icy with indignation, Mrs Thorn said, 'Haven't you ever seen a scarecrow before?'

I cried out desperately as if, even in the face of this evidence, I could still prove them wrong, 'But scarecrows are in fields!'

'Not in this part of the world.' Daniel's voice was thin and hoarse. He couldn't have looked more gaunt, more shocked, if it had really been Dennis Clifton in that tree. 'In this part of the world we put them in cherry trees. I put it there last night. I put *them* there.' And he pointed at what I had passed but never seen, the man in the tree by the wall, the man in the tree in the middle of the green lawn.

I went back to the house and up to my room and lay on the bed, prone and silent with shame. The next day was Saturday and my parents were coming. They would tell them and I should be taken home in disgrace. In the middle of the day Mrs Thorn came to the door and said to come down to lunch. She was a changed woman, hard and dour. I had never heard the expression 'to draw aside one's skirts' but later on when I did I recognized that this was what she had done to me. Her attitude to me was as if I were some sort of psychopath.

We had lunch alone, only I didn't really have any, I couldn't eat. Just as we were finishing, I pushing aside my laden plate, Daniel came in and sat down and said they had all talked about it and they thought it would be best if I went home with my parents on the following day.

'Of course I shall tell them exactly what you said and what you inferred,' said Mrs Thorn. 'I shall tell them how you insulted your auntie.'

Daniel, who wasn't trembling any more or any redder in the face than usual, considered this for a moment in silence. Then he said unexpectedly—or unexpectedly to me, 'No, we won't, Mother, we won't do that. No point in that. The fewer know the better. You've got to think of Ella's reputation.'

'I won't have her here,' his mother said.

'No, I agree with that. She can tell them she's homesick or I'll say it's too much for you, having her here.'

Ella hid herself away all that day.

'She has her letter to write to Philip,' said Mrs Thorn.

In the morning she was at the table with the others. Daniel made an announcement. He had been down to the village and heard that Dennis Clifton was back in the Air Force, he had rejoined his squadron.

'He'll soon be back in the thick of it,' he said.

Ella sat with bowed head, working with restless fingers a slice of bread into a heap of crumbs. Her face was colourless, lacking her usual make-up. I don't remember ever hearing another word from her.

I packed my things. My parents made no demur about taking me back with them. Starved of love, sickened by the love of others, I clung to my father. The scarecrows grinned at us as we got into the van behind Daniel. I can see them now—I can permit myself to see them now—spreadeagled in the trees, protecting the reddening fruit, so lifelike that even the swallows swooped in wider arcs around them.

* * *

In the following spring Ella died giving birth to another dead child. My mother cried, for Ella had been her little sister. But she was shy about giving open expression to her grief. She and my father were anxious to keep from me, or for that matter anyone else, that it was a good fifteen months since Philip Thorn had been home on leave. What became of Daniel and his mother I never knew, I didn't want to know. I couldn't avoid hearing that Philip had married again and his new wife was a niece of Mrs Leithman's.

★ ★ ★

Only a meticulous reader of newspapers would have spotted the paragraph. I am in the habit of reading every line, with the exception of the sports news, and I spotted this item tucked away between an account of sharp practice in local government and the suicide of a financier. I read it. The years fell away and the facts exonerated me. I knew I must do something, I wondered what, I have been thinking of it all day, but now I know I must tell this story to the coroner. My story, my mistake, Daniel's rage.

An agricultural worker had come upon an unexploded bomb on farm land near Inchfield in Suffolk. It was thought to be one of a stick of bombs dropped there in 1941. Excavations in the area had brought to light a skeleton thought to be that of a young man who had met his death at about the same time. A curious fact was that shotgun pellets had been found in the cavity of the skull.

The orchard walls are high and hard to climb.

And the place death considering who thou art, if any of my kinsmen find thee here . . .

HARE'S HOUSE

A murderer had lived in the house, the estate agent told Norman. The murder had in fact been committed there, he said. Norman thought it very open and honest of him.

'The neighbours would have mentioned it if I hadn't,' said the estate agent.

Now Norman understood why the house was going cheap. It was what they called a town house, though Norman didn't know why they did as he had seen plenty like it in the country. There were three floors and an open-tread staircase going up the centre. About fifteen years old, the estate agent said, and for twelve of those no one had lived in it.

'I'm afraid I can't give you any details of the case.'

'I wouldn't want to know,' said Norman. 'I'd rather not know.' He put his head round the door of the downstairs bathroom. He had never thought it possible he might own a house with more than one bathroom. Did he seriously consider owning this one then? The price was so absurdly low! 'What was his name?'

'The murderer? Oh, Hare. Raymond Hare.'

Rather to his relief, Norman couldn't remember any Hare murder case. 'Where is he now?'

'He died in prison. The house belongs to a nephew.'

'I like the house,' Norman said cautiously. 'I'll have to see what my wife says.'

The area his job obliged him to move into was a more prestigious one than where they now lived. A terraced cottage like the ones in Inverness Street was the best he had thought they could run to. He would never find another bargain like this one. If he hadn't been sure Rita would find out about the murder he would have avoided telling her.

'Why is it so cheap?' she said.

He told her.

She was a small thickset woman with brown hair and brown eyes and a rather large pointed face. She had a way of extending her neck and thrusting her face forward. It had once occurred to Norman that she looked like a mole, though moles of course could be attractive creatures. She thrust her head forward now.

'Is there something horrible you're not telling me?'

'I've told you everything I know. I don't know any details.' Norman was a patient and easy-going man, if inclined to be sullen. He was rather good-looking with a boyish open face and brown curly hair. 'We could both go and see it tomorrow.'

Rita would have preferred a terraced cottage in Inverness Street with a big garden and not so many stairs. But Norman had set his heart on the town house and was capable of sulking for months if he didn't get his own way. Besides, there was nothing to *show* Hare had lived there. Rather foolishly perhaps, Rita now thought, she had been expecting bloodstains or even a locked room.

'I've no recollection of this Hare at all, have you?'

'Let's keep it that way,' said Norman. 'You said yourself it's better not to know. I'll make Mr Hare the nephew an offer, shall I?'

The offer was accepted and Norman and Rita moved in at the end of September. The neighbours on one side had lived there eight years and the neighbours on the other six. They had never known Raymond Hare. A family called Lawrence who had lived in their large old house surrounded by garden for more than twenty years must have known him, at least by sight, but Norman and Rita had never spoken to them save to pass the time of day.

They had builders in to paint the house and they had new carpets. There were only two drawbacks and one of those was the stairs. You found yourself always running up and down to fetch things you had forgotten. The other drawback was the bathroom window, or more specifically, the catch on the bathroom window.

Sometimes, especially when Norman was at work and she was alone, Rita would wonder exactly where the murder had taken place. She would stand still, holding her duster, and look about her and think maybe it was in that room or that one or in their bedroom. And then she would go into the bedroom, thrusting her head forward and peering. Her mother used to say she had a 'funny feeling' in the corners of some houses, she said she was psychic. Rita would have liked to have inherited this gift but she had to admit she experienced no funny feelings in any part of this house.

She and Norman never spoke about Raymond Hare. They tended to avoid the very subject of murder. Rita had once enjoyed detective stories but somehow she didn't read them any more. It seemed better not to. Her next-door neighbour Dorothy, the one who had lived there eight years, tried one day to talk to her about the Hare case but Rita said she'd rather not discuss it.

'I quite understand,' Dorothy said. 'I think you're very wise.'

It was a warm house. The central heating was efficient and the windows were double glazed except for the one in the upstairs bathroom. This bathroom had a very high ceiling and the window was about ten feet up. It was in the middle of the house and therefore had no outside wall so the architect had made the roof of the bathroom just above the main roof, thus affording room for a window. It was a nuisance not being able to open it except by means of the pole with the hook on the end of it that stood against the bathroom wall, but the autumn was a dull wet one and the winter cold so for a long time there was no need to open the bathroom window at all.

Norman thought he would have a go at re-tiling the downstairs bathroom himself and went to the library to look for a do-it-yourself decorating manual. The library, a small branch, wasn't far away, being between his house and the tube station. Unable at first to find Skills and Crafts, his eye wandered down through Horticulture, Botany, Biology, General Science, Social Sciences, Crime . . .

Generally speaking, Norman had nothing to do with crime these days. He and Rita had even stopped watching thriller serials on television. His impulse was to turn his eyes sharply away from these accounts of trials and reconstructions of murders and turn them away he did but not before he had caught the name Hare on the spine of one of the books.

Norman turned his back. By a happy chance he was facing the section labelled 'Interior Decoration'. He found the book he wanted. Then he stood holding it and thinking. Should he look again? It might be that the author's name was Hare and had nothing at all to do with his Hare. Norman didn't really believe this. His stomach began to feel queasy and he was conscious of being rather excited too. He turned round and quickly took the book off the shelf. Its title was *Murder in the Sixties*, the author was someone called H. L. Robinson and the cases examined were listed on the jacket: Renzini and Boyce, The Oasthouse Mystery, Hare, The Pop Group Murders.

Norman opened it at random. He found he had opened it in the middle of the Hare case. A page or two further on were two photographs, the top one of a man with a blank characterless face and half-closed eyes, the other of a smiling fair-haired woman. The caption said that above was Raymond Henry Montagu Hare and below Diana Margaret Hare, née Kentwell. Norman closed the book and replaced it on the shelf. His heart was beating curiously hard. When his do-it-yourself book had been stamped he had to stop himself actually running out of the library. What a way to behave! he thought. I must get a grip on myself. Either I am going to put Hare entirely out of my mind and never think of him again or else I am going to act like a rational man, read up the case, make myself conversant with the facts and learn to live with them.

He did neither. He didn't visit the library again. When his book had taught him all it could about tiling he asked Rita to return it for him. He tried to put Hare out of his mind but this was too difficult. Where had he committed the murder was one of the questions he often asked himself and then he began to wonder whom he had killed and by what means. The answers were in a book on a shelf not a quarter of a mile away. Norman had to pass the library on his way to the station each morning and on his way back each night. He took to walking on the other side of the street. Sometimes there came into his mind that remark of Rita's that there might be something horrible he wasn't telling her.

Spring came early and there were some warm days in March. Rita tried to open the bathroom window, using the pole with the hook on the end, but the catch wouldn't budge. When Norman came home she got him to borrow a ladder from Dorothy's husband Roy and climb up and see what was wrong with the catch.

Norman thought Roy gave him rather a funny look when he said what he wanted the ladder for. He hesitated before saying Norman could have it.

'It's quite OK if you'd rather not,' Norman said. 'I expect I can manage with the steps if I can find a foothold somewhere.'

'No, no, you're welcome to the ladder,' said Roy and he showed Norman the bathroom in his own house which was identical with the next-door's except that the window had been changed for a blank sheet of glass with an extractor fan.

'Very nice,' said Norman, 'but just the same I'd rather have a window I can open.'

That brought another funny look from Roy.

Norman propped the ladder against the wall and climbed up to the window and saw why it wouldn't open. The two parts of the catch, a vertical bolt and a slot for it to be driven up into, had been wired together. Norman supposed that the builders doing the painting had wired up the window catch, though he couldn't imagine why. He undid the wire, slid down the bolt and let the window fall open to its maximum capacity of about seventy-five degrees.

* * *

On 1 April the temperature dropped to just on freezing and it snowed. Rita closed the bathroom window. She took hold of the pole, reached up and inserted the hook in the ring on the bottom of the bolt, lifted the window, closed it, pushed up the bolt into the slot and gave it a twist. When she came out of the bathroom on to the landing she stood looking about her and wondering where Hare had committed the murder. For a moment she fancied she had a funny feeling about that but it passed. Rita went down to the kitchen and made herself a cup of tea. She looked out into the tiny square of garden on to which fluffy snow was falling and melting when it touched the grass. There would have been room in the garden in Inverness Street to plant bulbs, daffodils and narcissi. Rita sighed. She poured out the tea and was stirring sugar into her cup when there came a loud crash from upstairs. Rita nearly jumped out of her skin.

She ran up the two flights of stairs, wondering what on earth had got broken. There was nothing. Nothing was out of place or changed. She had heard of haunted houses where loud crashes were due to poltergeist activity. Her mother had always been able to sense the presence of a poltergeist. She felt afraid and sweat broke out on her rather large pointed face. Then she noticed the bathroom door was closed. Had it been that door closing she had heard? Surely not. Rita opened the bathroom door and saw that the window had fallen open. So that was all it was. She got the pole and inserted the hook in the ring on the bolt, slid the bolt upwards into the slot and gave it a twist.

It had been rather windy but the wind had dropped. Next day the weather began to warm up again. Norman opened the bathroom window and it remained open until rain started. Rita closed it.

'That window's not the problem I thought it might be once you get the hang of using the pole,' said Norman.

He was trying to be cheerful and to act as if nothing had happened. The man called Lawrence who lived opposite had got into conversation with him on his way home. They had found themselves sitting next to each other in the tube train.

'It's good to see someone living in your place at last. An empty house always gets a run-down look.'

Norman just smiled. He had started to feel uneasy.

'My wife knew Mrs Hare quite well, you know.'

'Really?' said Norman.

'A nice woman. There was no reason for what he did as far as anyone could tell. But I imagine you've read it all up and come to terms with it. Well, you'd have to, wouldn't you?'

'Oh, yes,' said Norman.

Because he had his neighbour with him he couldn't cross the street to avoid passing the library. Outside its gates he had an almost intolerable urge to go in and take that book from the shelf. One thing he knew now, whether he wanted to or not, was that it was his wife Hare had murdered.

Some little while after midnight he was awakened by a crash. He sat up in bed.

'What was that?'

'The bathroom window, I expect,' said Rita, half-asleep.

Norman got up. He took the pole, inserted the hook into the ring on the bolt, slid up the bolt and gave it a firm clockwise twist. The rest of the night passed undisturbed. Rita opened the window two or three days later because it had turned warm. She went into their bedroom and changed the sheets and thought, for no reason as far as she could tell, I wonder if it was his wife he murdered? I expect it was his wife. Then she thought how terrible it would be if he had murdered her in bed. Hare's bed must have stood in the same place as their own. It must have because of the position of the electric points. Perhaps he had come home one night and murdered her in bed.

A wind that was more like a gale started to make the house cold. Rita closed the bathroom window. About an hour after Norman got home it blew open with a crash.

'It comes open,' said Norman after he had shut it, 'because when you close it you don't give the bolt a hard enough twist.'

'It comes open because of the wind,' said Rita.

'The wind wouldn't affect it if you shut it properly.' Norman's handsome face wore its petulant look and he sulked rather for the rest of the evening.

Next time the window was opened petals from fruit tree blossom blew in all over the dark blue carpet. Rita closed it an hour or so before Norman came home. Dorothy was downstairs having a cup of tea with her.

'I'd have that window wired up if I were you,' said Dorothy, and she added oddly, 'To be on the safe side.'

'It gets so hot in there.'

'Leave it open then and keep the door shut.'

The crash of the window opening awoke Norman at two in the morning. He was furious. He made a lot of noise about closing it in order to wake Rita.

'I told you that window wouldn't come open if you gave the bolt a hard enough twist. That crashing scares the hell out of me. My nerves can't stand it.'

'What's wrong with your nerves?'

Norman didn't answer. 'I don't know why you can't master a simple knack like that.'

'It isn't me, it's the wind.'

'Nonsense. Don't talk such nonsense. There is no wind.'

Rita opened the window in order to practise closing it. She spent about an hour opening and closing the window and giving the bolt a firm clockwise twist. While she was doing this she had a funny feeling. She had the feeling someone was standing behind and watching what she did. Of course there was no one there. Rita meant to leave the window open as it was a dry sunny day but she had closed it for perhaps the tenth time when the phone rang. The window therefore remained closed and Rita forgot about it.

She was pulling up weeds in the tiny strip of front garden when a woman who lived next door to the Lawrences came across the road, rattled a tin at her and asked for a donation for Cancer Research.

'I hope you don't mind my telling you how much I like your bedroom curtains.'

'Thank you very much,' said Rita.

'Mrs Hare had white net. Of course that was a few years back. You don't mind sleeping in that bedroom then? or do you use one of the back rooms?'

Rita's knees felt weak. She was speechless.

'I suppose it isn't as if he actually did the deed in the bedroom. More just outside on the landing, wasn't it?'

Rita gave her a pound to get rid of her. She went upstairs and stood on the landing and felt very funny indeed. Should she tell Norman? How could she tell him, how could she begin, when they had never once mentioned the subject since they moved in? Norman never thought about it anyway, she was sure of that. She watched him eating his supper as if he hadn't a care in the world. The window crashed open just as he was starting on his pudding. He jumped up with an angry shout.

'You're going to come with me into that bathroom and I'm going to teach you how to shut that window if it's the last thing I do!'

He stood behind her while she took the pole and inserted the hook into the ring on the bolt, pushed the bolt up and gave it a firm twist.

'There, you see, you've turned it the wrong

way. I said clockwise. Don't you know what clockwise means?'

Norman opened the window and made Rita close it again. This time she twisted the bolt to the right. The window crashed open before they had reached the foot of the stairs.

'It's not me, you see, it's the wind,' Rita cried.

Norman's voice shook with rage. 'The wind couldn't blow it open if you closed it properly. It doesn't blow it open when I close it.'

'You close it then and see. Go on, you do it.'

Norman closed it. The crash awakened him at three in the morning. He got up, cursing, and went into the bathroom. Rita woke up and jumped out of bed and followed him. Norman came out of the bathroom with the pole in his hand, his face red and his eyes bulging. He shouted at Rita:

'You got up after I was asleep and opened that window and closed it your way, didn't you?'

'I did *what*?'

'Don't deny it. You're trying to drive me mad with that window. You won't get the chance to do it again.'

He raised the pole and brought it down with a crash on the side of Rita's head. She gave a dreadful hoarse cry and put up her hands to try and ward of the rain of blows. Norman struck her five times with the pole and she was lying unconscious on the landing floor before he realized what he was doing. Norman threw the pole down the stairwell, picked Rita up in his arms and phoned for an ambulance.

* * *

Rita didn't die. She had a fractured skull and a broken jaw and collarbone but she would survive. When she regained consciousness and could move her jaw again she told the people at the hospital she had got up in the night and fallen over the banisters and all the way down the stairwell in the dark. The curious thing was she seemed to believe this herself.

Alone and remorseful, Norman kept thinking how odd it was there had nearly been a second murder under this roof. He went to the estate agents and told them he wanted to put the house back on the market. Hare's house, he always called it to himself these days, never 'my house' or 'ours'. They looked grave and shook their heads but brightened up when Norman named the very low figure he intended to ask.

Now he was going to be rid of the house Norman began to feel differently about Hare. He wouldn't have minded knowing what Hare had done, the details, the facts. One Saturday afternoon a prospective buyer came, was in raptures over Norman's redecorations and the tiles in the downstairs bathroom, and didn't seem to care at all about Hare. This encouraged

Norman and immediately the man had gone he went down the road to the library where he got out *Murder in the Sixties*. He read the account of the case after getting back from visiting Rita in hospital.

Raymond and Diana Hare had been an apparently happy couple. One morning their cleaner arrived to find Mrs Hare beaten to death and lying in her own blood on the top landing outside the bathroom door. Hare had soon confessed. He and his wife had had a midnight dispute over a window that continually came open with a crash and in the heat of anger he had attacked her with a wooden pole. Not a very interesting or memorable murder. Robinson, in his foreword, said he had included it among his four because what linked them all was a common lack of any kind of understandable motive.

But how could I have tried to do the same thing and for the same reason? Norman asked himself. Is Hare's house haunted by an act, by a motiveless urge? Or can it be that the first time I looked into that book I saw and read more than my conscious mind took in but not more than was absorbed by my *unconscious*? A rational man must believe the latter.

He borrowed the ladder from Roy to climb up and once more wire the window catch.

'By the way,' he said. 'I've been meaning to ask you. It's not the same pole, is it?'

'Your one, you mean? The same as Hare's? Oh, no, I don't know what became of that one. In some police museum, I expect. You've got ours. When we had our window done we offered ours to Mr Hare the nephew and he was very glad to accept.'

Norman found a buyer at last. Rita was away convalescing and he was obliged to find a new home for them in her absence. Not that he had much choicc, the miserable sum he got for Hare's house. He put a deposit on one of the terraced cottages in Inverness Street, hoping poor Rita wouldn't mind too much.

BRIBERY AND CORRUPTION

Everyone who makes a habit of dining out in London knows that Potters in Marylebone High Street is one of the most expensive of eating places. Nicholas Hawthorne, who usually dined in his rented room or in a steak house, was deceived by the humble-sounding name. When Annabel said, 'Let's go to Potters,' he agreed quite happily.

It was the first time he had taken her out. She was a small pretty girl with very little to say for herself. In her little face her eyes looked huge and appealing—a flying fox face, Nicholas thought. She suggested they take a taxi to Potters 'because it's difficult to find'. Seeing that it was a large building and right in the middle of Marylebone High Street, Nicholas didn't think it would have been more difficult to find on foot than in a taxi but he said nothing.

He was already wondering what this meal was going to cost. Potters was a grand and imposing restaurant. The windows were of that very clear but slightly warped glass that bespeaks age, and the doors of a dark red wood that looked as if it had been polished every day for fifty years. Because the curtains were drawn and the interior not visible, it appeared as if they were approaching some private residence, perhaps a rich man's town house.

Immediately inside the door was a bar where three couples sat about in black leather chairs. A waiter took Annabel's coat and they were conducted to a table in the restaurant. Nicholas, though young, was perceptive. He had expected Annabel to be made as shy and awkward by this place as he was himself but she seemed to have shed her diffidence with her coat. And when waiters approached with menus and thc winc list she said boldly that she would start with a Pernod.

What was it all going to cost? Nicholas looked unhappily at the prices and was thankful he had his newly acquired credit card with him. Live now, pay later—but, oh God, he would still have to pay.

Annabel chose asparagus for her first course and roast grouse for her second. The grouse was the most expensive item on the menu. Nicholas selected vegetable soup and a pork chop. He asked her if she would like red or white wine and she said one bottle wouldn't be enough, would it, so why not have one of each?

She didn't speak at all while they ate. He remembered reading in some poem or other how the poet marvelled of a schoolmaster that one small head could carry all he knew. Nicholas wondered how one small body could carry all Annabel ate. She devoured roast potatoes with her grouse and red cabbage and runner beans, and when she heard the waiter recommending braised artichokes to the people at the next table she said she would have some of those too. He prayed she wouldn't want another course. But that fawning insinuating waiter had to come up with the sweet trolley.

'We have fresh strawberries, madam.'

'In November?' said Annabel, breaking her silence. 'How lovely.'

Naturally she would have them. Drinking the dregs of his wine, Nicholas watched her eat the strawberries and cream and then call for a slice of chocolate roulade. He ordered coffee. Did sir and madam wish for a liqueur? Nicholas shook his head vehemently. Annabel said she would have a green chartreuse. Nicholas knew that this was of all liqueurs the pearl—and necessarily the most expensive.

By now he was so frightened about the bill and so repelled by her concentrated guzzling that he needed briefly to get away from her. It was plain she had come out with him only to stuff and drink herself into a stupor. He excused himself and went off in the direction of the men's room.

In order to reach it he had to pass across one end of the bar. The place was still half-empty but during the past hour—it was now nine o'clock—another couple had come in and were sitting at a table in the centre of the floor. The man was middle-aged with thick silver hair and a lightly tanned taut-skinned face. His right arm was round the shoulder of his companion, a very young, very pretty blond girl, and he was whispering something in her ear. Nicholas recognized him at once as the chairman of the company for which his own father had been sales manager until two years before when he had been made redundant on some specious pretext. The company was called Sorensen-McGill and the silver-haired man was Julius Sorensen.

With all the fervour of a young man loyal to a beloved parent, Nicholas hated him. But Nicholas was a very young man and it was beyond his strength to cut Sorensen. He muttered a stiff good evening and plunged for the men's room where he turned out his pockets, counted the notes in his wallet and tried to calculate what he already owed to the credit card company. If necessary he would have to borrow from his father, though he would hate to do that, knowing as he did that his father had been living on a reduced income ever since that beast Sorensen fired him. Borrow from his father, try and put off paying the rent for a month if he could, cut down on his smoking, maybe give up altogether . . .

When he came out, feeling almost sick, Sorensen and the girl had moved farther apart from each other. They didn't look at him and Nicholas too looked the other way. Annabel was on her second green chartreuse and gobbling up *petits fours*. He had thought her face was like that of a flying fox and now he remembered that flying fox is only a pretty name for a fruit bat. Eating a marzipan orange, she looked just like a rapacious little fruit bat. And she was very drunk.

'I feel ever so sleepy and strange,' she said. 'Maybe I've got one of those viruses. Could you pay the bill?'

It took Nicholas a long time to catch the waiter's eye. When he did the man merely homed in on them with the coffee pot. Nicholas surprised himself with his own firmness.

'I'd like the bill,' he said in the tone of one who declares to higher authority that he who is about to die salutes thee.

In half a minute the waiter was back. Would Nicholas be so good as to come with him and speak to the maître d'hôtel? Nicholas nodded, dumbfounded. What had happened? What had he done wrong? Annabel was slouching back in her chair, her big eyes half-closed, a trickle of something orange dribbling out of the corner of her mouth. They were going to tell him to remove her, that she had disgraced the place, not to come here again. He followed the waiter, his hands clenched.

A huge man spoke to him, a man with the beak and plumage of a king penguin. 'Your bill has been paid, sir.'

Nicholas stared. 'I don't know what you mean.'

'Your father paid it, sir. Those were my instructions, to tell you your father had settled your bill.'

The relief was tremendous. He seemed to grow tall again and light and free. It was as if someone had made him a present of—well, what would it have been? Sixty pounds? Seventy? And he understood at once. Sorensen had paid his bill and said he was his father. It was a little bit of compensation for what Sorensen had done in dismissing his father. He had paid out sixty pounds to show he meant well, to show that he wanted, in a small way, to make up for injustice.

Tall and free and masterful, Nicholas said, 'Call me a cab, please,' and then he went and shook Annabel awake in quite a lordly way.

His euphoria lasted for nearly an hour, long after he had pushed the somnolent Annabel through her own front door, then climbed the stairs up to the furnished room he rented and settled down to the crossword in the evening paper. Things would have turned out very different if he hadn't started that crossword. 'Twelve across: Bone in mixed byre goes with corruption. (7 letters)' Then I and the Y were already in. He got the answer after a few seconds—'Bribery'. 'Rib' in an anagram of 'byre'. 'Bribery'.

He laid down the paper and looked at the

opposite wall. That which goes with corruption. How could he ever have been such a fool, such a naive innocent fool, as to suppose a man like Sorensen cared about injustice or ever gave a thought to wrongful dismissal or even believed for a moment he *could* have been wrong? Of course Sorensen hadn't been trying to make restitution, of course he hadn't paid that bill out of kindness and remorse. He had paid it as a bribe.

He had paid the bribe to shut Nicholas's mouth because he didn't want anyone to know he had been out drinking with a girl, embracing a girl, who wasn't his wife. It was bribery, the bribery that went with corruption.

Once, about three years before, Nicholas had been with his parents to a party Sorensen had given for his staff and Mrs Sorensen had been the hostess. A brown-haired mousey little woman, he remembered her, and all of forty-five which seemed like old age to Nicholas. Sorensen had paid that bill because he didn't want his wife to find out he had a girlfriend young enough to be his daughter.

He had bought him, Nicholas thought, bribed and corrupted him—or tried to. Because he wasn't going to succeed. He needn't think he could kick the Hawthorne family around any more. Once was enough.

It had been nice thinking that he hadn't after all wasted more than half a week's wages on that horrible girl but honour was more important. Honour, surely, meant sacrificing material things for a principle. Nicholas had a bad night because he kept waking up and thinking of all the material things he would have to go short of during the next few weeks on account of his honour. Nevertheless, by the morning his resolve was fixed. Making sure he had his cheque book with him, he went off to work.

Several hours passed before he could get the courage together to phone Sorensen-McGill. What was he going to do if Sorensen refused to see him? If only he had a nice fat bank account with five hundred pounds in it he could make the grand gesture and send Sorensen a blank cheque accompanied by a curt and contemptuous letter.

The telephonist who used to answer in the days when he sometimes phoned his father at work answered now.

'Sorensen-McGill. Can I help you?'

His voice rather hoarse, Nicholas asked if he could have an appointment with Mr Sorensen that day on a matter of urgency. He was put through to Sorensen's secretary. There was a delay. Bells rang and switches clicked. The girl came back to the phone and Nicholas was sure she was going to say no.

'Mr Sorensen asks if one o'clock will suit you?'

In his lunch hour? Of course it would. But

what on earth could have induced Sorensen to have sacrificed one of those fat expense account lunches just to see him? Nicholas set off for Berkeley Square, wondering what had made the man so forthcoming. A weak hopeful little voice inside him began once again putting up those arguments which on the previous evening the voice of a common sense had so decisively refuted.

Perhaps Sorensen really meant well and when Nicholas got there would tell him the paying of the bill had been no bribery but a way of making a present to the son of a once-valued employee. The pretty girl could have been Sorensen's daughter. Nicholas had no idea if the man had children. It was possible he had a daughter. No corruption then, no betrayal of his honour, no need to give up cigarettes or abase himself before his landlord.

They knew him at Sorensen-McGill. He had been there with his father and, besides, he looked like his father. The pretty blond girl hadn't looked in the least like Sorensen. A secretary showed him into the chairman's office. Sorensen was sitting in a yellow leather chair behind a rosewood desk with an inlaid yellow leather top. There were Modigliani-like murals on the wall behind him and on the desk a dark green jade ashtray, stacked with stubs, which the secretary replaced with a clean one of pale green jade.

'Hallo, Nicholas,' said Sorensen. He didn't smile. 'Sit down.'

The only other chair in the room was one of those hi-tech low-slung affairs made of leather hung on a metal frame. Beside it was a black glass coffee table with a black leather padded rim and on the glass lay a magazine open at the centrefold of a nude girl. There are some people who know how to put others at their ease and there are those who know how to put others in difficulties. Nicholas sat down, right down—about three inches from the floor.

Sorensen lit a cigarette. He didn't offer the box. He looked at Nicholas and moved his head slowly from side to side. At last he said:

'I suppose I should have expected this.'

Nicholas opened his mouth to speak but Sorensen held up his hand. 'No, you can have your say in a minute.' His tone became hard and brisk. 'The girl you saw me with last night was someone—not to put too fine a point on it—I picked up in a bar. I have never seen her before, I shall never see her again. She is not, in any sense of the words, a girlfriend or mistress. Wait,' he said as Nicholas again tried to interrupt. 'Let me finish. My wife is not a well woman. Were she to find out where I was last night and whom I was with she would doubtless be very distressed. She would very likely become ill again. I refer, of course, to mental illness, to an emotional sickness, but . . .'

He drew deeply on his cigarette. 'But all this being so and whatever the consequences, I shall not on any account allow myself to be blackmailed. Is that understood? I paid for your dinner last night and that is enough. I do not want my wife told what you saw, but you may tell her and publish it to the world before I pay you another penny.'

At the word blackmail Nicholas's heart had begun to pound. The blood rushed into his face. He had come to vindicate his honour and his motive had been foully misunderstood. In a choked voice he stuttered:

'You've no business—it wasn't—why do you say things like that to me?'

'It's not a nice word, is it? But to call it anything else would merely be semantics. You came, didn't you, to ask for more?'

Nicholas jumped up. 'I came to give you your money back!'

'Aah!' It was a strange sound Sorensen made, old and urbane, cynical yet wondering. He crushed out his cigarette. 'I see. Youth is moralistic. Inexperience is puritanical. You'll tell her anyway because you can't be bought, is that it?'

'No, I can't be bought.' Nicholas was trembling. He put his hands down flat on Sorensen's desk but still they shook. 'I shall never tell anyone what I saw, I promise you that. But I can't let you pay for my dinner—and pretend to be my father!' Tears were pricking the backs of his eyes.

'Oh, sit down, sit down. If you aren't trying to blackmail me and your lips are sealed, what the hell did you come here for? A social call? A man-to-man chat about the ladies you and I took out last night? Your family aren't exactly my favourite companions, you know.'

Nicholas retreated a little. He felt the man's power. It was thc power of money and the power that is achieved by always having had money. There was something he hadn't ever before noticed about Sorensen but which he noticed now. Sorensen looked as if he were made of metal, his skin of copper, his hair of silver, his suit of pewter.

And then the mist in Nicholas's eyes stopped him seeing anything but a blur. 'How much was my bill?' he managed to say.

'Oh, for God's sake.'

'How much?'

'Sixty-seven pounds,' said Sorensen, 'give or take a little.' He sounded amused.

To Nicholas it was a small fortune. He got out his cheque book and wrote the cheque to J. Sorensen and passed it across the desk and said, 'There's your money. But you needn't worry. I won't say I saw you. I promise I won't.'

Uttering those words made him feel noble, heroic. The threatening tears receded. Sorensen looked at the cheque and tore it in two.

'You're a very tiresome boy. I don't want you on my premises. Get out.'

Nicholas got out. He walked out of the building with his head in the air. He was still considering sending Sorensen another cheque when, two mornings later, reading his paper in the train, his eye caught the hated name. At first he didn't think the story referred to 'his' Sorensen—and then he knew it did. The headline read: 'Woman Found Dead in Forest. Murder of Tycoon's Wife.'

'The body of a woman,' ran the story beneath,

> was found last night in an abandoned car in Hatfield Forest in Hertfordshire. She had been strangled. The woman was today identified as Mrs Winifred Sorensen, 45, of Eaton Place, Belgravia. She was the wife of Julius Sorensen, chairman of Sorensen-McGill, manufacturers of office equipment.
>
> Mrs Sorensen had been staying with her mother, Mrs Mary Clifford, at Mrs Clifford's home in Much Hadham. Mrs Clifford said, 'My daughter had intended to stay with me for a further two days. I was surprised when she said she would drive home to London on Tuesday evening.'
>
> 'I was not expecting my wife home on Tuesday,' said Mr Sorensen. 'I had no idea she had left her mother's house until I phoned

there yesterday. When I realized she was missing I immediately informed the police.'

Police are treating the case as murder.

That poor woman, thought Nicholas. While she had been driving home to her husband, longing for him probably, needing his company and his comfort, he had been philandering with a girl he had picked up, a girl whose surname he didn't even know. He must now be overcome with remorse. Nicholas hoped it was biting agonized remorse. The contrast was what was so shocking, Sorensen cheek to cheek with that girl, drinking with her, no doubt later sleeping with her; his wife alone, struggling with an attacker in a lonely place in the dark.

Nicholas, of course, wouldn't have been surprised if Sorensen had done it himself. Nothing Sorensen could do would have surprised him. The man was capable of any iniquity. Only this he couldn't have done, which none knew better than Nicholas. So it was a bit of a shock to be accosted by two policemen when he arrived home that evening. They were waiting in a car outside his gate and they got out as he approached.

'Nothing to worry about, Mr Hawthorne,' said the older of them who introduced himself as a Detective Inspector. 'Just a matter of routine. Perhaps you read about the death of Mrs Winifred Sorensen in your paper today?'

'Yes.'

'May we come in?'

They followed him upstairs. What could they want of him? Nicholas sometimes read detective stories and it occurred to him that, knowing perhaps of his tenuous connection with Sorensen-McGill, they would want to ask him questions about Sorensen's character and domestic life. In that case they had come to the right witness.

He could tell them all right. He could tell them why poor Mrs Sorensen, jealous and suspicious as she must have been, had taken it into her head to leave her mother's house two days early and drive home. Because she had intended to catch her husband in the act. And she would have caught him, found him absent or maybe entertaining that girl in their home, only she had never got home. Some maniac had hitched a lift from her first. Oh yes, he'd tell them!

In his room they sat down. They had to sit on the bed for there was only one chair.

'It has been established,' said the Inspector, 'that Mrs Sorensen was killed between eight and ten p.m. on Tuesday.'

Nicholas nodded. He could hardly contain his excitement. What a shock it was going to be for them when he told them about this supposedly respectable businessman's private life! A split second later Nicholas was left deflated and staring.

'At nine that evening Mr Julius Sorensen, her husband, was in a restaurant called Potters in Marylebone High Street accompanied by a young lady. He had made a statement to us to that effect.'

Sorensen had told them. He had confessed. The disappointment was acute.

'I believe you were also in the restaurant at that time?'

In a small voice Nicholas said, 'Oh yes. Yes, I was.'

'On the following day, Mr Hawthorne, you went to the offices of Sorensen-McGill where a conversation took place between you and Mr Sorensen. Will you tell me what that conversation was about, please?'

'It was about my seeing him in Potters the night before. He wanted me to . . .' Nicholas stopped. He blushed.

'Just a moment, sir. I think I can guess why you're so obviously uneasy about this. If I may say so without giving offence you're a very young man as yet and young people are often a bit confused when it comes to questions of loyalty. Am I right?'

Mystified now, Nicholas nodded.

'Your duty is plain. It's to tell the truth. Will you do that?'

'Yes, of course.'

'Good. Did Mr Sorensen try to bribe you?'

'Yes.' Nicholas took a deep breath. 'I made him a promise.'

'Which must carry no weight, Mr Hawthorne. Let me repeat. Mrs Sorensen was killed between eight and ten. Mr Sorensen has told us he was in Potters at nine, in the bar. The bar staff can't remember him. The surname of the lady he says he was with is unknown to him. According to him you were there and you saw him.' The Inspector glanced at his companion, then back to Nicholas. 'Well, Mr Hawthorne? This is a matter of the utmost seriousness.'

Nicholas understood. Excitement welled in him once more but he didn't show it. They would realize why he hesitated. At last he said:

'I was in Potters from eight till about nine-thirty.' Carefully he kept to the exact truth. 'Mr Sorensen and I discussed my being there and seeing him when I kept my appointment with him in his office on Wednesday and he—he paid the bill for my dinner.'

'I see.' How sharp were the Inspector's eyes! How much he thought he knew of youth and age, wisdom and naivety, innocence and corruption! 'Now then—did you in fact see Mr Sorensen in Potters on Tuesday evening?'

'I can't forget my promise,' said Nicholas.

Of course he couldn't. He had only to keep his promise and the police would charge

Sorensen with murder. He looked down. He spoke in a guilty troubled voice.

'I didn't see him. Of course I didn't.'

THE WHISTLER

Jeremy found the key in one of the holiday flats while he was working for Manuel. The flats were being painted throughout in a colour called champagne and so far they hadn't found a machine to do this. Jeremy hoped they wouldn't until the job was done. Manuel was an American citizen though he came from somewhere south of the border—Cuba, Jeremy had always supposed. Jeremy himself came from somewhere a long way north of the border, England in fact, and he had been feeling his way around the United States for a couple of years now, always hoping for his luck to change. The key, he thought, might be a piece of luck.

It was up in a corner of the bedroom windowsill, under the blind. Manuel was in the living room, whistling country music. He whistled all the time he was working, never anything Spanish, always Western or country stuff, and he never played the radio which Jeremy would have preferred. The key had a label tied on its head with a piece of string. On the label an address was written. Jeremy started to say, or thought of saying, 'Hey, Manuel, look at this . . .' and then checked himself. The whistling went on unbroken. Whatever might be on offer at the address on the key label, did he want to have to share it with Manuel? Or, worse, did he want Manuel to take the key off him?

Finding things in the flats wasn't unusual. People were very careless. They rented these flats at Juanillo Beach for a couple of weeks in the high season and went off home to New Jersey or Moscow, Idaho, or wherever it might be, leaving their jewellery behind and their cameras, not to mention such trifles as books and tapes and so on. The company who owned the property were supposed to come in and check before Manuel started but they didn't make much of a job of it. Jeremy had found a roll of banknotes, over eighty dollars, in a kitchen unit, and in a gap between tiled floor and wall, a diamond ring. A jeweller in downtown Miami had given him $250 for the ring and that was probably a fraction of its value. It had been a mistake telling Manuel about it. Manuel hadn't cared about the banknotes but he had jibbed at the ring. It wasn't that he was more honest than the next man, but he had this contract with Juanillo Beach Properties Inc. and he didn't want to lose it. At any rate he had warned Jeremy off helping himself to anything he found in the flats—which was enough in itself to make Jeremy pick up the key and put it in the pocket of his jeans. In the next room the whistling continued, becoming very rollicking and Rocky Mountain.

It was starting to get hot and the air conditioning had broken down. Or Juanillo Beach Properties had taken the fuse out, Jeremy thought. He wouldn't put it past them. By noon it would be up in the nineties. Well, it was for the climate he'd come down here and for the climate he stayed. It is easier to be poor in a warm climate. He thought of England with horror, of being deported and having to go back there as his worse nightmare. It couldn't really be like that, it wasn't, but he remembered his native land as green and cold, full of rich elderly people who had log fires going all the year round, a land of joblessness and privilege where, though he had been born there, he had never felt welcome. Now the blind was up he could see the subtropical garden in which the apartment block was, palms and citrus and Indian paintbrush and oleander and here and there the sliced spear leaves of a banana. Yellow and black striped zebra butterflies flitted among the thick shiny leaves. And the sun blazed from a clear blue sky. It suited him here, or would if he had a bit of money.

In London he had had a very small room, for which he paid £25 a week, and had shared bathroom and kitchen two floors down with four other tenants. Here he had a motel room with bath—well, shower—for less than that. And he didn't need a kitchen because eating out was cheap. But sometimes he thought he'd come to the United States too late to seek his fortune, maybe fifty years too late. That was what Josh who owned the motel said. Josh didn't know he was there illegally of course. Or if he did he didn't say.

After work he and Josh sometimes had a beer together on the porch at the rear of the motel office building. The motel was in a rough area and was pretty shabby but if there was one thing Josh kept in repair it was the screens round that porch. All the mosquitos of the diaspora came down there, Josh said, driven out of more prosperous parts.

Jeremy remembered the address on the key. 'Where's Eleventh Avenue?'

There were two more cans of Coors on the table, sweating icy drops, and a bag of toasted pecans. A little brown lizard ran up the screen on the outside.

'What d'you mean, Eleventh Avenue? Eleventh Avenue where?'

'Miami.'

'There's not so many cities in this country you'll find the avenues numbered. Streets, yes. Why? What d'you ask for?' He didn't wait for an answer. 'Take L.A., take Philly—they don't have numbered avenues.'

'New York has.'

'New York's different,' said Josh which was something Americans always said, Jeremy had noticed.

'So how about Miami?'

'Sure Miami's got an Eleventh Avenue. Downtown. There's a street plan in the office.'

Jeremy had a look at it. The address on the key was 1562A Ave. 11. No city, no state. The label was rather smudged and there had been more of the address there, a couple of capital letters, in fact. The second letter was certainly a J or a Y. Y for York? J for Juanillo? He knew without enquiring that there was no First Avenue in Juanillo, let alone Eleventh. Come to that, could he be sure the writer had meant Eleventh Avenue? Ave. 11 was a funny way of putting it, more a European way, except that Europeans don't number their streets much.

It wasn't likely to be Miami. People from Miami wouldn't rent a flat at Juanillo Beach. But he could try. Burglary would be so simple, scarcely dishonest even, when you didn't have to break in. That evening he was going to eat out with Manuel and Lupe in a Thai restaurant out in posh Fort Cayne where Manuel lived. But first he'd make a little trip downtown and try the key on the front door of 1562A Eleventh Avenue.

The place wasn't guarded, all was quiet. He rang the bell, waited, rang again, tried the key. It didn't fit. In the taxi going out to Fort Cayne he thought about what Josh had said about not many American cities having numbered avenues. Of course Josh might be wrong, he had only named three cities... Wasn't it more probable anyway that the key opened an apartment in New York? What was Eleventh Avenue, New York, like and how far uptown would 1562A be? If it was 1562 Fifth they were talking about he'd have some idea. He imagined a gorgeous New York apartment full of treasures waiting for someone to walk in and take them. The trouble was that the fare to New York was something around $300 round trip.

The restaurant was called the Phumiphol and it was in one of those glossy malls. Jeremy got there first and ordered a vodka on the rocks. Put it on the check, please. It was going to be a bit awkward meeting Lupe again. Nothing he couldn't handle, of course, but he did need that vodka.

Her real name was Guadelupe or Maria del Guadelupe or some such thing and she was an illegal immigrant like him. A small dark beautiful girl with the huge eyes and symmetrical features of those Mexican film stars of thirties Hollywood. She resembled a photograph he had seen of Dolores del Rio. Manuel was going to marry her and she too would become an American, as much a citizen as the President's wife or a Daughter or the American Revolution.

The vodka came and a little dish of something that looked like salted beetles but couldn't be. Jeremy had first met Lupe in Manuel's apartment. Not that she lived there with him. Manuel was very strict and very Spanish about that sort of thing. His affianced wife had to be a virgin and manifestly seen by all the world to be a virgin.

Oddly enough, Lupe had been. Jeremy had never actually come across one before. She lived in a room in a Cuban lady's house and every day she came to clean Manuel's apartment for him and iron his shirts. Manuel put his shirts through the washer himself but Lupe ironed them. Wherever she came from she didn't want to go back there and that, Jeremy had been sure, was why she was waiting on and obeying Manuel in the hope of marrying him. Manuel was an ugly devil, very thin and somehow spiderlike with a pockmarked hatchet face while Jeremy was tall, blond and good-looking which was partly, no doubt, why Lupe had fallen in love with him.

Or whatever you called it. At any rate she hadn't resisted much. Manuel had had to go home because his father was dying. He died before Manuel got there, so he was only away two days but that was enough. Jeremy and Lupe were making love in the apartment at Hacienda Alameda before Manuel got on the plane. Lupe's virginity was a surprise and bit daunting but after the third or fourth time it was all the same as if it had been gone five years.

The trouble was that they couldn't stop and at

last Manuel found out. One stupid afternoon when Jeremy had the day off and Lupe was cleaning the apartment they forgot discretion and succumbed. They might so easily have gone to the motel, he thought afterwards. Manuel didn't find them, nothing so crude as that, he found a blond hair and a long chestnut wavy hair on the pillow where only a black-haired man slept.

Jeremy was finishing off his vodka when Manuel and Lupe came in. Manuel looked cheerful and pleased with himself, talking about the holiday he would take away from Florida when the really hot weather started. Make it a honeymoon, was what Jeremy would have said a few months back. They say Alaska's a great place in the summer. Something stopped him saying it now. Manuel hadn't mentioned marriage since that night.

They had some transparent soup with flowers floating in it. A jar of sake and a bottle of Perrier water. Neither Manuel nor Lupe drank much. Then came little pancakes, shredded vegetables, perfumed duck. It was all as if dolls had cooked it. Lupe ate daintily, chewing every mouthful twenty times, keeping her head bent.

'I want to act like a civilized man,' Manuel had said, and pathetically, Jeremy thought, 'Like an American gentleman.' He looked ridiculous when he was unhappy, a black crow with mud on its feathers. 'My ancestors would have killed you and her too.'

Jeremy had cast up his eyes at that. Oh, Christ . . .

'Times have changed. With me it will be as if it had never happened.' Manuel looked at Lupe. 'But it must never happen again.'

'It won't happen again,' said Lupe.

'Of course not.' Jeremy didn't want her any more anyway. All this fuss was enough to put one off more desirable women than Lupe Garcia.

'Then you stay working for me,' Manuel said to Jeremy, 'and bygones shall be bygones.' He smiled. He insisted on shaking Jeremy's hand. Then he went to the kitchen to open a bottle of wine, whistling 'The Tennessee Waltz' as he went. An apposite if tactless choice, Jeremy thought, but perhaps Manuel didn't know the words. Lupe tried to catch his eyes but Jeremy wouldn't look.

That had been two months ago and this was the first time since then that he had seen Lupe. It was archaic the feeling the whole set-up gave him that by that one initial act, let alone the others, he had spoiled her for Manuel, she was damaged goods. She had grown more subdued. She didn't look unhappy. They ate little cakes of dough in syrup sauce.

Manuel had his car, though he lived only round the corner. Jeremy was asked back for coffee. He went to the bathroom and saw unmistakable signs of Lupe's occupancy, a jar of skinfood, an eyeliner, a bottle of the cologne she used. It hadn't taken long for Manuel's principles to break down, Jeremy thought with a quiet laugh to himself.

'Yes, I've moved in,' she said to him.

He looked at her hand and she saw him looking. Not even an engagement ring.

Manuel drove him home. He had just taken delivery of this year's new car. Jeremy often wondered where the money came from. You didn't own a condominium at prestigious Hacienda Alameda and have a new car every year and fly home to see your family every couple of months out of painting ceilings. It was no business of his. He'd be moving on soon anyway. Maybe to California when he could raise the fare.

The coconut palms round Josh's Motel hummed with tree frogs as if they themselves were sensate things, an unbroken droning that twitched at the nerves. They kept Jeremy awake. He could go to New York instead and try out that key. There were two letters on that label after Ave. 11 and one of them could be a Y. Perhaps there were only two cities in the United States with numbered avenues—and perhaps there were dozens.

A couple of days later he and Manuel moved on into the next apartment. It was the same as the one they had finished except that no one had left a key on the window sill. Manuel was whistling away in the next room, a song about the sunflowers of Kansas. He had taken off the fancy pale blue blouson he had been wearing and slung it down over the side of the bath. There was nowhere else to put it. Jeremy felt in the pockets. He had done this before when times were hard and hauled himself fifty bucks. Manuel was too careless about money to notice. The whistling continued, only the tune changing and going south to become 'The Yellow Rose of Texas'. Jeremy pulled out a wad of notes, all of them twenties, a lot of money.

He couldn't just pocket it, that was no good. He looked about him, thinking quickly. The bath plug was the metal kind, operated by a level underneath the taps but nevertheless removable. Jeremy removed it and carefully poked the roll of notes inside. The roll expanded a little to fit the hole as he had known it would. He put the plug back.

Manuel or he usually went out at lunchtime and fetched back a couple of Whoppers, onion rings and two Cokes. It was Manuel who always paid. Cutting off the whistling, he went to the bathroom for his jacket and the six or seven dollars Jeremy would need at Burger King. This time he wasn't quite so philosophical about the loss of his money.

'I know you're not accusing me,' Jeremy said. 'I know you wouldn't do that, but for my own sake I'd like to show you.'

He pulled the empty pockets out of his jeans, stripped off his shirt, kicked off his shoes, handed Manuel his own denim jacket with just $8 in the pocket.

'I don't know how much you had on you, Manuel, but you were swinging that thing around when we got in the car at my place. It's a rough old area round Josh's . . .'

'And finding's keepings, eh?' Manuel used a lot of quaint old English expressions that sounded crazy uttered in his Spanish accent. 'There's worse things happen at sea,' he said. 'But you may pay for the lunch.' He laughed and patted Jeremy on the back.

Jeremy hooked the notes out of the plughole before he went home. There were sixteen of them, more than enough to get to New York on. But suppose the place the key opened wasn't in New York? He'd have wasted all that money. It was an expensive looking key, a *classy* key, he thought, shinier, heavier, more trimly cut, than the keys that opened Hacienda Alameda . . .

Manuel went off home the following week and Lupe was alone. There was no way Jeremy was going to get himself involved with her again. He intended to avoid Fort Cayne altogether for the four days Manuel was gone.

She came to him. He was sitting out on the porch with Josh when she drove on to the parking lot in Manuel's new car. There was something uncertain and vulnerable in the way she drove, the way she parked. She had the lowest self-image of anyone Jeremy knew. Because she thought of herself as dirt people treated her like it, though physically she was obsessively clean, had two showers or baths every day. It was Oriental not Latin girls that had been compared to little flowers but Lupe reminded one of a flower, a hibiscus maybe.

'I should be so lucky,' said Josh.

'Help yourself.' Jeremy shrugged. Lupe had opened the screen door and was coming hesitantly up the steps. 'There's a new rule here,' he said to her. 'No members of the opposite sex in guests' rooms after sunset,' and he laughed at his own wit.

Her face grew hot. Josh who usually had a great sense of humour didn't laugh for some reason but asked her to sit down and how about a drink on the house? Lupe said quietly that she'd have a Coke if there was one. Josh brought the Coke and asked where Manuel was. He had once or twice met Manuel.

'San José,' said Lupe.

That did surprise Jeremy. 'His mum lives in California? I never knew that.'

'Not California, Costa Rica,' Josh said. 'Isn't that right? The capital of Costa Rica?'

She nodded. Jeremy barely knew where Costa Rica was and cared less. Josh said he'd never been there but he'd heard it didn't have an army and it was the only real democracy in Central America. Lupe hadn't been there either. Nicaragua was where she came from. They were actually having a conversation. Let's keep it that way, Jeremy thought.

He didn't know if she was devoted to Manuel or only to his money and his citizenship. Whichever it was, she talked about him all the time. He was a devoted son to his mother, he'd bought her a house in the best residential suburb of San José. Lupe had photographs which she proceeded to show them of a bungalow covered in bougainvillea with gilded bars on its windows.

Jeremy looked at the photographs which had been done by a professional whose address was stamped on the back. Ave. 2, it said, San José, Costa Rica.

★ ★ ★

From a bookshop in downtown Miami he managed to get a street plan of San José. It was a city in which the streets or *calles* were numbered and so were the avenues or *avenidas*. 'Ave.', of course, could be short for *avenida* as well as avenue. A grid-plan city more or less, with the avenues running east to west and the *calles* north to south. At Juanillo Beach Properties they told him that one of the apartments had last been occupied by a couple from Costa Rica. A lot of

Costa Ricans came to Florida for a week or a few days. Shopping was cheaper and better here. Electrical goods, for instance, were half the price they were in San José. But no, they couldn't give him the address. If he had found something in the flat let them have it and they'd send it on. Jeremy handed over a couple of rolls of film he'd bought just now at Gray Drug. The Juanillo Beach Properties girl looked at him as if he was out of his mind.

The travel agent he went to could get him a three-day package to San José for a lot less than he'd nicked off Manuel. Manuel was back by now and they were on the last apartment in the block. When Jeremy said he'd like next week off Manuel didn't put up any objections and seemed interested when he said he was going to New York. He smiled and patted Jeremy's shoulder and said something about the Big Apple and in a funny old-fashioned phrase, not to do anything he, Manuel, wouldn't do. Then he took a clean brush and the bucket of emulsion and went off into the bedroom whistling that song about a boy called Sue.

Jeremy got there in the late afternoon. There were more Costa Ricans than Americans on the flight and when the captain announced they were beginning their descent for San José they all clapped and cheered and drummed their feet. Evidently they were a patriotic lot. A bus the tour company had laid on took him into the city.

It was four thousand feet up and cooler than Florida though a lot nearer the equator. There was a view of blue mountains behind coffee plantations and banana groves and the whole was dotted with flame-of-the-forest trees like points of fire. Jeremy had seen a bit of the Third World one way and another and immediately outside the city he expected to see the shantytowns of poverty, the huts made of tin and sacks and plastic bags, the rubbish tips and flies. Poverty didn't bother him, he never thought about it, but here in a kind of subconscious way he expected to see it just as in his native land he expected rain and Tudor mansions, but there was none to be seen. Only neat stucco bungalows and little houses like on an English council estate.

In case the plan had lied it was a comfort to see the *avenidas*. The Hotel Latinoamericana was on Avenida Central and if it wasn't exactly the Hilton it was the best hotel Jeremy had ever stayed in and about five stars up on Josh's. The dark came down at six o'clock. Carmen the tour guide had warned them about pickpockets in the city where thieves abounded. Jeremy thought he would have an early night. San José did anyway, the hotel bar closing at ten sharp.

In the morning he swam in the hotel pool. The water was icy. Outside in the Avenida Central the atmosphere was thick and stinking with petrol fumes. He walked downtown a bit but the pollution which hung as blue smog and obscured the mountains made him cough. Another thing Carmen had said was that if you took a taxi you should settle the fare with the driver first. Jeremy found a taxi and haggled a bit but he had no Spanish and the driver hardly any English and when he had seated himself in the back he was fairly certain he'd be ripped off. The driver was going to take him on a city tour.

First they went to the suburb on the road to Irazu where the finest houses were and the foreign embassies. It wasn't Avenida 11 nor was Manuel's mother's house to be seen. The driver pointed out places of interest that Jeremy wasn't interested in. He showed him the university and the museum of art and then, not far from the children's hospital, Jeremy did see a bungalow very like Manuel's mother's, perhaps indeed the very one, with orange bougainvillea swarming all over it, a golden grille to keep out the burglars and a little white dog peering out of one of the windows. At one point they actually drove along Avenida 11 but nowhere near number 1562. It wasn't far from the Latinoamericana though, he could easily walk there.

After dark? That might be best. Or should he watch the house or flat or whatever it was for the occupants to go out? He remembered that after all he had only two days. He paid the taxi driver—twice, it seemed to him, what they had fixed on—and walked up the Calle Central to

Avenida 11. There were two branches of it, the street being broken rather ominously by the Central Prison.

When he found thc house he was deeply disappointed. It wasn't even up to the standard of Manuel's mother's place, far below it in fact. He thought of where his parents lived in London, in North Finchley. This bungalow, standing alone on the side of the road, might itself have been in North Finchley but for the two palm trees in front of it and the thorn hedge with red flowers which divided it from the abandoned lot stacked with empty oil drums next door.

Lace curtains, none too clean, hung at all the windows. The paint was faded. It looked unoccupied but he didn't dare try the key. He walked across the oil drum lot and looked round the back. Everything shut up. An empty dog kennel and a broken rusty dog chain.

Hc found a McDonald's and lunched there. The unaccustomed high altitude was tiring and after a few drinks in the hotel bar he slept. By six-thirty it was quite dark. He walked up the Calle Central onto Avenida 11 and back to the bungalow. It was in darkness, not a light on in the place. The traffic was beginning to thin and with it the smog so that it was possible now to see the stars and a wire-thin curve of moon. He stood on the opposite side of the street and watched the house. For a quarter of an hour he did that. He went round the back across the oil drum lot and looked round the rear. Nothing. No one. Darkness. There were fewer people on the street now. He walked away, as far as the zoo, back again along a nearly deserted street, breathing clean fresh air. The house looked just the same. He took the key out of his pocket, walked up to the front door and inserted it in the lock. The door opened easily.

He closed it behind him and stood in the small square hall. The place smelt dusty, stuffy, breath-catching as places do that have been shut up a long time in a warm dry climate. Not only was it unoccupied now, it had been unoccupied for months. A little light came in from the street but not enough. Jeremy switched on his torch. He pushed open a door and found himself in a bedroom, insufferably stuffy, smelling of camphor. By the marks on the walls he could see that pieces of furniture had been removed from it and only the big bed with carved mahogany headboard and white lace cover remained. The bungalow was a sizeable house, much bigger than it seemed from outside. There were two more bedrooms, one empty of furniture. Either the traffic on Avenida 11 had ceased or you couldn't hear it in here. He moved through the rooms in dim musty silence, directing the torch beam across walls and floors.

The front room or parlour was also half-furnished. There had been a piano or chest of drawers up against one wall. Shabby wooden-armed chairs stood around. The wallpaper was stained and yellow, imprinted with small paler rectangles where framed photographs had once hung. One still remained, hanging crookedly, a family group.

There was nothing worth taking. The most valuable thing was probably the hand-crocheted lace bed cover which, when he looked at it again, turned out to be scored by the depredations of moths. He returned to the living room. There was a drawer in the table which he didn't expect to contain the family silver or wads of whatever they called their currency, *colones*, but he might as well look. It didn't. He was right. The drawer had two paper table napkins in it and a United States ten cent piece, a dime. Closing the drawer, he raised the beam of the torch and it fell on the single framed photograph. Something made Jeremy look more closely, bringing the light right up to the glass.

He gasped as if a hand had fallen on his shoulder. The picture was of an old wrinkle-faced man and a stout old woman with three young men standing behind them, one of them spidery thin, very dark, sharp-featured. Jeremy looked and shut his eyes and looked again. He thought, I have to get out of here and fast. It may be too late. There may be someone in the house now, he may have been here all the time, one of those brothers . . .

He put out the torch. He listened. There was only the dark dusty silence. He went out into the hall, his heart beating quickly, sweat standing on his forehead. When he opened the front door . . . But he dared not open it. A window? The back way was obviously the worst idea. It was dark, desolate, empty at the rear. Though Avenida 11 seemed deserted the front door was still his best bet. He ought to have a weapon. A poker? It was never cold enough in this country to have a fire. He groped his way into the kitchen, opened the door and yelled aloud, clamping his hand too late over his mouth.

Something tall and thin was standing in an embrasure of the wall between sink and cupboard. He didn't know what he'd imagined but when he shone the torch on it he saw it was a six-foot-tall houseplant in a tub, dried-up, brown, dead. There was a piece of iron pipe with a tap on it lying on the draining board. Jeremy took it with him.

Gripping his weapon in his right hand, he opened the front door with his left. There was no one there, no sound, no still or moving shadow. A car with only side lights on cruised slowly down Avenida 11 and turned into a side street. The ten minutes it took Jeremy to get out of the neighbourhood and find a taxi were some of the worst he had ever spent. He knew one of Manuel's brothers had to be lying in wait for him in a doorway or else following him until he reached a totally dark and secluded part of the road.

The house he had been in had obviously once been the home of Manuel's parents. It was probably now up for sale. Manuel had of course moved his mother somewhere more plush. Jeremy could see it all, how he had been led here, but he didn't let himself think too much about the ins and outs of it until at last a taxi came and he was safely in it. No haggling about fares this time.

Why had Manuel done it? Because Jeremy had stolen $320 from him, no doubt. Anyway, it hadn't come off. Perhaps he had gone to the house in Avenida 11 earlier or later than they'd expected or one of those brothers had got the date wrong. Or it might even be that Manuel's desire to get his own back would be satisfied by Jeremy's disappointment at finding nothing to steal in the house. For Manuel might only be hoaxing him, merely playing a *joke*.

Jeremy felt relieved at this idea. If Manuel's aim had simply been to teach him a lesson—well, that was OK with him. He'd been taught a lesson. If he ever saw another key lying about he'd leave it where it was. But his fear was ebbing with every turn the taxi took to bring him nearer the Latinoamericana. It was all right, he was safe now, he could even see the funny side of it—the irony of getting nothing out of the burgled house but an old iron tap.

At the desk he asked for his key. The reception clerk said Jeremy hadn't handed it in, so Jeremy felt in his pockets but it wasn't there. He had a hollow feeling first that he had had the key and his pocket had been picked, then that someone must have come into the hotel while he was out and taken the key from the pigeon-hole. It could very easily be done by reaching across the end of the counter while the clerk had his back turned or was attending to another guest.

The clerk found a second key to his room and sent the wizened old bellboy up with him. The door was locked. The bellboy bent over and picked something up from the floor, something that had been half-hidden by the bottom of the door.

'Here is your key, señor.'

Jeremy was beginning to hate the sight of keys. He sent the man away. Was it possible he had dropped the key there himself? As soon as he was inside he knew there was no question of that. The room had been turned upside down. What he had planned to do, he thought, they had done to him. He sat down in the wicker chair and surveyed the mess. His bedding was in a heap, the mattress doubled over and half on the floor. All the drawers in the dressing table-cum-writing desk had been pulled out. He hadn't brought much luggage with him, a zipper bag only, but they had taken everything out of it and strewn the contents, spare pair of jeans, sweat shirt, sponge bag, half-bottle of duty-free Kahlua, across the floor. But nothing had been damaged or destroyed. There was nothing missing—or was there?

An empty envelope lay half under the sweat shirt. Jeremy read what was written on it and remembered. 'Fond thoughts from Lupe.' He had told her that wasn't the way to write it. You should say 'love from' or 'best wishes from'. Inside had been a cassette of Latin-American love songs, awful stuff he'd never even bothered to take out of the zipper bag he'd had with him that weekend at Hacienda Alameda . . .

And obviously he never had taken it out. He had repacked the bag with the cassette—wrapped in red tissue paper, he recalled, sealed in this envelope—still inside. Well, if it was that tape they wanted they were welcome to it. But why should they want it? Jeremy hauled the mattress back on to the bed. He felt horribly uneasy, his hands shook and a muscle twitched in his forehead. He could have done with a drink but the bar closed at ten and it was past that. He pulled the stopper off the Kahlua bottle and then thought: suppose they put something in it?

Had the whole exercise been mounted simply to get back a tape Lupe had given him? No, of course not. It wasn't being done because he'd stolen the $320 either, he saw that now. It was because he'd stolen Lupe. Manuel had probably *meant* him to steal the money, had indeed set it up. It wasn't normal for a man, however well off, to be quite so careless with cash as that or indifferent to its loss . . .

Jeremy was too frightened now not to drink the Kahlua. It enabled him to get some sleep. First, though, he pulled the heavy writing desk across the door. A sound he thought came from in the room awakened him and he jumped up with a cry, but it wasn't in the room, it was outside in the corridor, the people next door coming in late. A Kahlua hangover began to bash his head. He had no aspirin and dared not leave the room to go and ask for some.

Thank God he was going back to Miami today. He didn't leave the hotel. He breakfasted in the dining room, despite the cost, and sat for the rest of the morning on the leather settee facing reception and reading one of the few books in English the Latinoamericana had, a James M. Cain paperback. Nothing untoward happened. He jumped out of his skin when a voice uttered his name into his ear. It was only Carmen, the tour guide.

'The bus for the international airport is going thirteen hundred hours. Have a nice day!'

Could he go back and work for Manuel again? The chances were Manuel wouldn't say a word, would want bygones to be bygones, in his own phrase. Jeremy thought he'd work for him just long enough to get the fare together for California ... It was a long three hours before the bus came. He'd finished *The Postman Always Rings Twice* and was reduced to reading travel brochures. He didn't bother with lunch. It was only something else that cost money.

* * *

Nobody drummed feet or clapped when the aircraft began its descent for Miami. But Jeremy felt a lightening of his heart. For one thing, Immigration would doubtless allow him a further six months' stay in the United States. His last six months' allowance had long since expired but he'd torn the slip out of his passport and would say it had fallen out and got lost. That was a trick he'd used successfully coming over the border from Mexico once before. Feeling you were legal even for a little while gave you a sense of security.

He walked into Customs. They tended to search young people coming in after a short stay in Central or South America. Josh had told him. So he wasn't concerned when the Customs man took everything out of the zipper bag and only mildly surprised at the close examination his sponge bag was subjected to.

There was a split in the bottom seam. The Customs man put his fingers through, then his whole hand, and drew out from between cover and lining a package wrapped in red tissue paper. The red tissue, which he'd last seen round Lupe's cassette, unfolded to reveal its contents, a fine white crystalline powder.

Jeremy had never seen it before but he knew what it was. He thought briefly of the annual new car, of Hacienda Alameda, and then he thought of himself and how he need not worry about his stay in the United State being curtailed. He would be there a long time.

THE CONVOLVULUS CLOCK

'Is that your own hair, dear?'

Sibyl only laughed. She made a roguish face.

'I didn't think it could be,' said Trixie. 'It looks so thick.'

'A woman came up to me in the street the other day,' said Sibyl, 'and asked me where I had my hair set. I just looked at her. I gave a tiny little tip to my wig like this. You should have seen her face.'

She gave another roar of laughter. Trixie smiled austerely. She had come to stay with Sibyl for a week and this was her first evening. Sibyl had bought a cottage in Devonshire. It was two years since Trixie had seen Sibyl and she could detect signs of deterioration. What a pity that was! Sibyl enquired after the welfare of the friends they had in common. How was Mivvy? Did Trixie see anything of the Fishers? How was Poppy?

'Poppy is beginning to go a bit funny,' said Trixie.

'How do you mean, "funny"?'

'You know. Funny. Not quite *compos mentis* any more.'

Sibyl of all people ought to know what going funny meant, thought Trixie.

'We're none of us getting any younger,' said

Sibyl, laughing.

Trixie didn't sleep very well. She got up at five and had her bath so as to leave the bathroom clear for Sibyl. At seven she took Sibyl a cup of tea. She gave a little scream and nearly dropped the tray.

'Oh my conscience! I'm sorry, dear, but I thought that was a squirrel on your chest of drawers. I thought it must have come in through the window.'

'What on earth was that noise in the middle of the night?' When Sibyl wasn't laughing she could be downright peevish. She looked a hundred without her wig. 'It woke me up, I thought the tank was overflowing.'

'The middle of the night! I like that. The sun had been up a good hour, I'm sure. I was just having my bath so as not to be a nuisance.'

They went out in Sibyl's car. They had lunch in Dawlish and tea in Exmouth. The following day they went out early and drove across Dartmoor. When they got back there was a letter on the mat for Trixie from Mivvy, though Trixie had only been away two days. On Friday Sibyl said they would stay at home and have a potter about the village. The church was famous, the Manor House gardens were open to the public and there was an interesting small gallery where an exhibition was on. She started to get the car out but Trixie said why couldn't they walk. It could hardly be more than a mile.

Sibyl said it was just under two miles but she agreed to walk if Trixie really wanted to. Her knee hadn't been troubling her quite so much lately.

'The gallery is called Artifacts,' said Sibyl. 'It's run by a very nice young couple.'

'A husband and wife team?' asked Trixie, very modern.

'Jimmy and Judy they're called. I don't think they are actually married.'

'Oh my conscience, Sibyl, how can one be "actually" married? Surely one is either married or not?' Trixie herself had been married once, long ago, for a short time. Sibyl had never been married and neither had Mivvy or Poppy. Trixie thought that might have something to do with their going funny. 'Thankfully, I'm broad-minded. I shan't say anything. I think I can see a seat ahead in that bus shelter. Would you like a little sit-down before we go on?'

Sibyl got her breath back and they walked on more slowly. The road passed between high hedges on high banks dense with wild flowers. It crossed a stream by a hump-backed bridge where the clear brown shallow water rippled over a bed of stones. The church appeared with granite nave and tower, standing on an eminence and approached, Sibyl said, by fifty-three steps. Perhaps they should to Artifacts first?

The gallery was housed in an ancient building

with bow windows and a front door set under a Georgian portico. When the door was pushed open a bell tinkled to summon Jimmy or Judy. This morning, however, they needed no summoning for both were in the first room, Judy dusting the dolls' house and Jimmy doing something to the ceiling spotlights. Sibyl introduced Trixie to them and Trixie was very gracious towards Judy, making no difference in her manner than she would have if the young woman had been properly married and worn a wedding ring.

Trixie was agreeably surprised by the objects in the exhibition and by the items Jimmy and Judy had for sale. She had not expected such a high standard. What she admired most particularly were the small pictures of domestic interiors done in embroidery, the patchwork quilts and the blown glass vases in colours of mother-of-pearl and butterfly wings. What she liked best of all and wanted to have was a clock.

There were four of these clocks, all different. The cases were ceramic, plain and smooth or made in a trellis work, glazed in blues and greens, painted with flowers or the moon and stars, each incorporating a gilt-rimmed face and quartz movement. Trixie's favourite was blue with a green trellis over the blue, a convolvulus plant with green leaves and pale pink trumpet flowers climbing the trellis and a gilt rim round the face of the clock which had hands of gilt and blue. The convolvulus reminded her of the pattern on her best china tea service. All the clocks had price cards beside them and red discs stuck to the cards.

'I should like to buy this clock,' Trixie said to Judy.

'I'm terribly sorry but it's sold.'

'Sold?'

'All the clocks were sold at the private view. Roland Elm's work is tremendously popular. He can't make enough of these clocks and he refuses to take orders.'

'I still don't understand why I can't buy this one,' said Trixie. 'This is a shop, isn't it?'

Sibyl had put on her peevish look. 'You can see the red sticker, can't you? You know what that means.'

'I know what it means at the Royal Academy but hardly here surely.'

'I really do wish I could sell it to you,' said Judy, 'but I can't.'

Trixie lifted her shoulders. She was very disappointed and wished she hadn't come. She had been going to buy Sibyl a pear carved from polished pear wood but now she thought better of it. The church also was a let-down, dark, poky and smelling of mould.

'Things have come to a pretty pass when shopkeepers won't sell their goods to you because they're upset by your manner.'

'Judy wasn't upset by your manner,' said

Sibyl, puffing. 'It's more than her reputation is worth to sell you something she's already sold.'

'Reputation! I like that.'

'I mean reputation as a gallery owner. Artifacts is quite highly regarded round here.'

'You would have thought she and her—well, partner, would be glad of £62. I don't suppose they have two half-pennies to bless themselves with.'

What Sibyl would have thought was never known for she was too out of breath to utter and when they got home had to lie down. Next morning another letter came from Mivvy.

'Nothing to say for herself of course,' said Trixie at breakfast. 'Practically a carbon copy of Thursday's. She's going very funny. Do you know she told me sometimes she writes fifty letters in a week? God bless your pocket, I said. It's fortunate you can afford it.'

They went to Princetown in Sibyl's car and Widecombe-in-the-Moor. Trixie sent postcards to Mivvy, Poppy, the Fishers and the woman who came in to clean and water the plants in the greenhouse. She would have to buy some sort of present for Sibyl before she left. A plant would have done, only Sibyl didn't like gardening. They went to a bird sanctuary and looked at some standing stones of great antiquity. Trixie was going home on Tuesday afternoon. On Tuesday morning another letter arrived from Mivvy all about the Fishers going to see the

Queen Mother open a new arts centre in Leighton Buzzard. The Fishers were crazy about the Queen Mother, watched for her engagements in advance and went wherever she went within a radius of 150 miles in order just to catch a glimpse of her. Once they had been at the front of the crowd and the Queen Mother had shaken hands with Dorothy Fisher.

'We're none of us getting any younger,' said Sibyl, giggling.

'Well, my conscience, I know one thing,' said Trixie. 'The days have simply flown past while I've been here.'

'I'm glad you've enjoyed yourself.'

'Oh, I have, dear, only it would please me to see you a little less frail.'

Trixie walked to the village on her own. Since she couldn't think of anything else she was going to have to buy the pear-wood pear for Sibyl. It was a warm sunny morning, one of the best days she'd had, and the front door of Artifacts stood open to the street. The exhibition was still on and the clocks (and their red 'sold' discs) still there. A shaft of sunlight streamed across the patchwork quilts on to the Georgian dolls' house. There was no sign of Jimmy and Judy. The gallery was empty but for herself.

Trixie closed the door and opened it to make the bell ring. She picked up one of the pear-wood pears and held it out in front of her on the palm of her hand. She held it at arm's length the way she did when she had helped herself to an item in the supermarket just so that there couldn't be the slightest question of anyone suspecting her of shoplifting. No one came. Trixie climbed the stairs, holding the pear-wood pear out in front of her and clearing her throat to attract attention. There was no one upstairs. A blue Persian cat lay sleeping on a shelf between a ginger jar and a mug with an owl on it. Trixie descended. She closed the front door and opened it to make the bell ring. Jimmy and Judy must be a heedless pair, she thought. Anyone could walk in here and steal the lot.

Of course she could just take the pear-wood pear and leave a £5 note to pay for it. It cost £4.75. Why should she make Jimmy and Judy a present of 25p just because they were too idle to serve her? Then she remembered that when she had been here with Sibyl a door at the end of the passage had been open and through that door one could see the garden where there was a display of terracotta pots. It was probable Jimmy and Judy were out there, showing the pots to a customer.

Trixie went through the second room and down the passage. The door to the garden was just ajar and she pushed it open. On the lawn, in a cane chair, Judy lay fast asleep. A ledger had fallen off her lap and lay on the grass alongside a heap of books. Guides to the management of tax they were and some which looked like the gallery account books. It reminded Trixie of Poppy who was always falling asleep in the daytime, most embarrassingly sometimes, at the table or even while waiting for a bus. Judy had fallen asleep over her book-keeping. Trixie coughed. She said 'Excuse me' very loudly and repeated it but Judy didn't stir.

What a way to run a business! It would serve them right if someone walked in and cleared their shop. It would teach them a lesson. Trixie pulled the door closed behind her. She found herself tiptoeing as she walked back along the passage and through the second room. In the first room she took the ceramic clock with the convolvulus on it off the shelf and put it into her bag and she took the card too with the red sticker on it so as not to attract attention to the clock's absence. The pear-wood pear she replaced among the other carved fruit.

The street outside seemed deserted. Trixie's heart was beating rather fast. She went across the road into the little newsagent's and gift shop and bought Sibyl a teacloth with a map of Devonshire on it. At the door, as she was coming out again, she saw Jimmy coming along the street towards the gallery with a bag of groceries under one arm and two pints of milk in the other. Trixie stayed where she was until he had gone into Artifacts.

She didn't much fancy the walk back but

there was no help for it. When she got to the bridge over the stream she heard hooves behind her and for a second or two had a feeling she was pursued by men on horseback but it was only a girl who passed her, riding a fat white pony. Sibyl laughed when she saw the teacloth and said it was a funny thing to give someone who *lived* in Devonshire. Trixie felt nervous and couldn't eat her lunch. Jimmy and Judy would have missed the clock by now and the newsagent would have remembered a furtive-looking woman skulking in his doorway and described her to them and soon the police would come. If only Sibyl would hurry with the car! She moved so slowly, time had no meaning for her. At this rate Trixie wouldn't even catch her train at Exeter.

She did catch it—just. Sibyl's car had been followed for several miles of the way by police in a Rover with a blue lamp on top and Trixie's heart had been in her mouth. Why had she done it? What had possessed her to take something she hadn't paid for, she who when shopping in supermarkets held 17p pots of yogurt at arm's length?

Now she was safely in the train rushing towards Paddington she began to see things in a different light. She would have paid for that clock if they had let her. What did they expect if they refused to sell things they had on sale? And what *could* they expect if they went to sleep leaving their shop unattended? For a few moments she had a nasty little qualm that the police might be waiting for her outside her own door but they weren't. Inside all was as it should be, all was as she had left it except that Poppy had put a pint of milk in the fridge and someone had arranged dahlias in a vase—not Poppy, she wouldn't know a dahlia from a runner bean.

That would be just the place for the clock, on the wall bracket where at present stood a photograph of herself and Dorothy Fisher at Broadstairs in 1949. Trixie put the photograph away in a drawer and the clock where the photograph had been. It looked nice. It transformed a rather dull corner of the room. Trixie put one of the cups from her tea service beside it and it was amazing how well they matched.

Mivvy came round first thing in the morning. Before letting her in Trixie quickly snatched the clock off the shelf and thrust it inside the drawer with the photograph. It seemed so *exposed* up there, it seemed to tell its history in every tiny tick.

'How did you find Sibyl?'

Trixie wanted to say, I went in the train to Exeter and got out at the station and there was Sibyl waiting for me in her car . . . Only if you started mocking poor Mivvy where would you end? 'Very frail, dear. I thought she was going a bit funny.'

'I must drop her a line.'

Mivvy always spoke as if her letters held curative properties. Receiving one of them would set you up for the winter. After she had gone Trixie considered replacing the clock on the shelf but thought better of it. Let it stay in the drawer for a bit. She had read of South American millionaires who have Old Masters stolen for them which they can never show but are obliged, for fear of discovery, to keep hidden away for ever in dark vaults.

Just before Christmas a letter came from Sibyl. They always sent each other Christmas letters. As Trixie said, if you can't get around to writing the rest of the year, at least you can at Christmas. Mivvy wrote hundreds. Sibyl didn't mention the theft of the clock or indeed mention the gallery at all. Trixie wondered why not. The clock was still in the drawer. Sometimes she lay awake in the night thinking about it, fancying she could hear its tick through the solid mahogany of the drawer, through the ceiling and the bedroom floorboards.

It was curious how she had taken a dislike to the convolvulus tea service. One day she found herself wrapping it in tissue paper and putting it away in the cupboard under the stairs. She took down all the trellis work round the front door and put up wires for the clematis instead. In March she wrote to Sibyl to enquire if there was a new exhibition on at Artifacts. Sibyl didn't answer for weeks. When she did she told Trixie that months and months back one of those ceramic clocks had been stolen from the gallery and a few days later an embroidered picture had also gone and furniture out of the dolls' house. Hadn't Sibyl mentioned it before? She thought she had but she was getting so forgetful these days.

Trixie took the clock out of the drawer and put it on the shelf. Because she knew she couldn't be found out she began to feel she hadn't done anything wrong. The Fishers were bringing Poppy round for a cup of tea. Trixie started unpacking the convolvulus tea service. She lost her nerve when she heard Gordon Fisher's car door slam and she put the clock away again. If she were caught now she might get blamed for the theft of the picture and the dolls' house furniture as well. They would say she had sold those things and how could she prove she hadn't?

Poppy fell asleep halfway through her second buttered scone.

'She gets funnier every time I see her,' Trixie said. 'Sad, really. Sibyl's breaking up too. She'll forget her own name next. You should see her letters. I'll just show you the last one.' She remembered she couldn't do that, it wouldn't be wise, so she had to pretend she'd mislaid it.

'Will you be going down there again this year, dear?' said Dorothy.

'Oh, I expect so. You know how it is, you get to the stage of thinking it may be the last time.'

Poppy woke up with a snort, said she hadn't been asleep and finished her scone.

Gordon asked Trixie, 'Would you like to come with us and see Her Majesty open the new leisure complex in Rayleigh on Monday?'

Trixie declined. The Fishers went off to do their shopping, leaving Poppy behind. She was asleep again. She slept till six and, waking, asked Trixie if she had put something in her tea. It was most unusual, she said, for her to nod off like that. Trixie walked her back to the bus stop because the traffic whipped along there so fast you had to have your wits about you and drivers didn't respect zebra crossings the way they used to. Trixie marched across on the stripes, confident as a lollipop lady but without the lollipop, taking her life in her hands instead.

She wrote to Sibyl that she would come to Devonshire at the end of July, thinking that while there it might be best to make some excuse to avoid going near Artifacts. The clock was still in the drawer but wrapped up now in a piece of old flannel. Trixie had taken a dislike to seeing the colour of it each time she opened the drawer. She had a summer dress that colour and she wondered why she had ever bought it, it didn't flatter her, whatever it might do for the Queen Mother. Dorothy could have it for her next jumble sale.

Walking back from posting a letter, Mivvy fell over and broke her ankle. It was weeks getting back to normal. Well, you had to face it, it was never going to be *normal*. You wouldn't be exaggerating, Trixie wrote to Sibyl, if you said that obsession of hers for writing letters had crippled her for life. Sibyl wrote back to say she was looking forward to the last week of July and what did Trixie think had happened? They had caught the thief of the pieces from Artifacts trying to sell the picture to a dealer in Plymouth. He had said in court he hadn't taken the clock but you could imagine how much credence the magistrate placed on that!

Trixie unwrapped the clock and put it on the shelf. Next day she got the china out. She wondered why she had been so precipitate in pulling all that trellis off the wall, it looked a lot better than strands of wire on metal hooks. Mivvy came round in a taxi, hobbling up the path on two sticks, refusing the offer of the taxi driver's arm.

'You'll be off to Sibyl's in a day or two, will you, dear?'

Trixie didn't know how many times she had told her not till Monday week. She was waiting for Mivvy to notice the clock but at this rate she was going to have to wait till Christmas.

'What do you think of my clock?'

'What, up there? Isn't that your Wedgwood coffee pot, dear?'

Trixie had to get it down. She thrust it under Mivvy's nose and started explaining what it was.

But Mivvy knew already. 'Of course I know it's a clock, dear. It's not the first time I've seen one of these. Oh my goodness, no. The young man who makes these, he's a friend of my nephew Tony, they were at art school together. Let me see, what's his name? It will come to me in a minute. A tree, isn't it? Oak? Ash? Peter Oak? No, Elm is his name. Something Elm. Roland Elm.'

Trixie said nothing. The glazed surface of the clock felt very cold against the skin of her hands.

'He never makes them to order, you know. He just makes a limited number for a few selected galleries. Tony told me that. Where did you get yours, I wonder?'

Trixie said nothing. There was worse coming and she waited for it.

'Not around here, I'm sure. I know there are only two or three places in the country they go to. It will come to me in a minute. I shall be writing to Tony tomorrow and I'll mention about you having one of Richard's—no, I mean Raymond's, that is, Roland's, clocks. I always write to him on Tuesdays. Tuesday is his day. I'll mention you've got one with bindweed on it. They're all different, you know. He never makes two alike.'

'It's convolvulus, not bindweed,' said Trixie.

'I'd rather you didn't write to Tony about it if you don't mind.'

'Oh, but I'd like to mention it, dear. Whyever not? I won't mention your name if you don't want me to. I'll just say that lady who goes down to stay with Auntie Sibyl in Devonshire.'

Trixie said she would walk with Mivvy up to the High Street. It was hopeless trying to get a taxi outside here. She fetched Mivvy's two sticks.

'You take my arm and I'll hold your other stick.'

The traffic whipped along over the zebra crossing. You were at the mercy of those drivers, Trixie said, it was a matter of waiting till they condescended to stop.

'Don't you set foot on those stripes till they stop,' she said to Mivvy.

Mivvy didn't, so the cars didn't stop. A container lorry, a juggernaut, came thundering along, but a good way off still. Trixie thought it was going much too fast.

'Now if we're quick,' she said. 'Run for it!'

Startled by the urgency in her voice, Mivvy obeyed, or tried to obey as Trixie dropped her arm and gave her a little push forward. The lorry's brakes screamed like people being tortured and Trixie jumped back, screaming herself, covering her face with her hands so as not to see Mivvy under those giant wheels.

* * *

Dorothy Fisher said she quite understood Trixie would still want to go to Sibyl's for her holiday. It was the best thing in the world for her, a rest, a complete change, a chance to forget. Trixie went down by train on the day after the funeral. She had the clock in her bag with her, wrapped first in tissue paper and then in her sky-blue dress. The first opportunity that offered itself she would take the clock back to Artifacts and replace it on the shelf she had taken it from. This shouldn't be too difficult. The clock was a dangerous possession, she could see that, like one of those notorious diamonds that carry a curse with them. Pretty though it was, it was an *unlucky* clock that had involved her in trouble from the time she had first taken it.

There was no question of walking to Artifacts this time. Sibyl was too frail for that. She had gone downhill a lot since last year and symptomatic of her deterioration was her exchange of the grey wig for a lilac-blue one. They went in the car though Trixie was by no means sure Sibyl was safe at the wheel.

As soon as they walked into the gallery Trixie saw that she had no hope of replacing the clock without being spotted. There was a desk in the first room now with a plump smiling lady sitting at it who Sibyl said was Judy's mother. Trixie thought that amazing—a mother not minding her daughter cohabiting with a man she wasn't married to. Living with a daughter living in sin, you might put it. Jimmy was in the second room, up on a ladder doing something to the window catch.

'They're having upstairs remodelled,' said Sibyl. 'You can't go up there.' And when Trixie tried to make her way towards the garden door, 'You don't want to be had up for trespassing, do you?' She winked at Judy's mother. 'We're none of us getting any younger when all's said and done, are we?'

They went back to Sibyl's, the clock still in Trixie's bag. It seemed to have grown heavier. She could hear it ticking through the leather and the folds of the sky-blue dress. In the afternoon when Sibyl lay down on the sofa for her rest, the lilac wig stuck on top of a Poole pottery vase, Trixie went out for a walk, taking the clock with her. She came to the hump-backed bridge over the stream where the water was very low, for it had been a dry summer. She unwrapped the clock and dropped it over the low parapet into the water. It cracked but the trellis work and the convolvulus remained intact and the movement continued to move and to tick as well for all Trixie knew. The blue and green, the pink flowers and the gilt, gleamed through the water like some exotic iridescent shell.

Trixie went down the bank. She took off her shoes and waded into the water. It was surprisingly cold. She picked up a large flat stone and beat at the face of the clock with it. She beat with unrestrained fury, gasping and grunting at each blow. The green trellis and the blue sky, the glass face and the pink flowers, all shattered. But they were still there, bright jewel-like shards, for all to see who came this way across the bridge.

Squatting down, Trixie scooped up handfuls of pebbles and buried the pieces of clock under them. With her nails she dug a pit in the bed of the stream and pushed the coloured fragments into it, covering them with pebbles. Her hands were bleeding, her knees were bruised and her dress was wet. In spite of her efforts the bed of the stream was still spread with ceramic chips and broken glass and pieces of gilt metal. Trixie began to sob and crawl from side to side of the stream, ploughing her hands through the blue and green and gold gravel, and it was there that one of Sibyl's neighbours found her as he was driving home over the bridge.

He lifted her up and carried her to his car.

'Tick-tock,' said Trixie. 'Tick-tock. Convolvulus clock.'

LOOPY

At the end of the last performance, after the curtain calls, Red Riding Hood put me on a lead and with the rest of the company we went across to the pub. No one had taken make-up off or changed, there was no time for that before The George closed. I remember prancing across the road and growling at someone on a bicycle. They loved me in the pub—well, some of them loved me. Quite a lot were embarrassed. The funny thing was that I should have been embarrassed myself if I had been one of them. I should have ignored *me* and drunk up my drink and left. Except that it is unlikely I would have been in a pub at all. Normally, I never went near such places. But inside the wolf skin it was very different, everything was different in there.

I prowled about for a while, sometimes on all fours, though this is not easy for us who are accustomed to the upright stance, sometimes loping, with my forepaws held close up to my chest. I went up to tables where people were sitting and snuffled my snout at their packets of crisps. If they were smoking I growled and waved my paws in air-clearing gestures. Lots of them were forthcoming, stroking me and making jokes or pretending terror at my red jaws and wicked little eyes. There was even one lady who took hold of my head and laid it in her lap.

Bounding up to the bar to collect my small dry sherry, I heard Bill Harkness (the First Woodcutter) say to Susan Hayes (Red Riding Hood's Mother):

'Old Colin's really come out of his shell tonight.'

And Susan, bless her, said, 'He's a real actor, isn't he?'

I was one of the few members of our company who was. I expect this is always true in amateur dramatics. There are one or two real actors, people who could have made their livings on the stage if it was not so overcrowded a profession, and the rest who just come for the fun of it and the social side. Did I ever consider the stage seriously? My father had been a civil servant, both my grandfathers in the ICS. As far back as I can remember it was taken for granted I should get my degree and go into the civil service. I never questioned it. If you have a mother like mine, one in a million, more a friend than a parent, you never feel the need to rebel. Besides, Mother gave me all the support I could have wished for in my acting. Acting as a hobby, that is. For instance, though the company made provision for hiring all the more complicated costumes for that year's Christmas pantomime, Mother made the wolf suit for me herself. It was ten times better than anything we could have hired. The head we had to buy but the body and the limbs she made from a long-haired grey fur fabric such as is manufactured for ladies' coats.

Moira used to say I enjoyed acting so much because it enabled me to lose myself and become, for a while, someone else. She said I disliked what I was and looked for ways of escape. A strange way to talk to the man you intend to marry! But before I approach the subject of Moira or, indeed, continue with this account, I should explain what its purpose is. The psychiatrist attached to this place or who visits it (I am not entirely clear which), one Dr Vernon-Peak, has asked me to write down some of my feelings and impressions. That, I said, would only be possible in the context of a narrative. Very well, he said, he had no objection. What will become of it when finished I hardly know. Will it constitute a statement to be used in court? Or will it enter Dr Vernon-Peak's files as another 'case history'? It is all the same to me. I can only tell the truth.

After The George closed, then, we took off our makeup and changed and went our several ways home. Mother was waiting up for me. This was not invariably her habit. If I told her I should be late and to go to bed at her usual time she always did so. But I, quite naturally, was not averse to a welcome when I got home, particularly after a triumph like that one.

Besides, I had been looking forward to telling her what an amusing time I had had in the pub.

Our house is late Victorian, double-fronted, of grey limestone, by no means beautiful, but a comfortable well-built place. My grandfather bought it when he retired and came home from India in 1920. Mother was ten at the time, so she has spent most of her life in that house.

Grandfather was quite a famous shot and used to go big game hunting before that kind of thing became, and rightly so, very much frowned upon. The result was that the place was full of 'trophies of the chase'. While Grandfather was alive, and he lived to a great age, we had no choice but to put up with the antlers and tusks that sprouted everywhere out of the walls, the elephant's foot umbrella stand, and the snarling maws of *tigris* and *ursa*. We had to grin and bear it, as Mother, who has a fine turn of wit, used to put it. But when Grandfather was at last gathered to his ancestors, reverently and without the least disrespect to him, we took down all those heads and horns and packed them away in trunks. The fur rugs, however, we did not disturb. These days they are worth a fortune and I always felt that the tiger skins scattered across the hall parquet, the snow leopard draped across the back of the sofa and the bear into whose fur one could bury one's toes before the fire, gave to the place a luxurious look. I took off my shoes, I remember, and snuggled my toes in it that night.

Mother, of course, had been to see the show. She had come on the first night and seen me make my onslaught on Red Riding Hood, an attack so sudden and unexpected that the whole audience had jumped to its feet and gasped. (In our version we did not have the wolf actually devour Red Riding Hood. Unanimously, we agreed this would hardly have been the thing at Christmas.) Mother, however, wanted to see me wearing her creation once more, so I put it on and did some prancing and growling for her benefit. Again I noticed how curiously uninhibited I became once inside the wolf skin. For instance, I bounded up to the snow leopard and began snarling at it. I boxed at its great grey-white face and made playful bites at its ears. Down on all fours I went and pounced on the bear, fighting it, actually forcing its neck within the space of my jaws.

How Mother laughed! She said it was as good as anything in the panto and a good deal better than anything they put on the television.

'Animal crackers in my soup,' she said, wiping her eyes. 'There used to be a song that went like that in my youth. How did it go on? Something about lions and tigers loop the loop.'

'Well, *lupus* means a wolf in Latin,' I said.

'And you're certainly loopy! When you put that suit on I shall have to say you're going all loopy again!'

When I put that suit on again. Did I intend to put it on again? I had not really thought about it. Yes, perhaps if I ever went to a fancy-dress party, a remote enough contingency. Yet what a shame it seemed to waste it, to pack it away like Grandfather's tusks and antlers, after all the labour Mother had put into it. That night I hung it up in my wardrobe and I remember how strange I felt when I took if off that second time, more naked than I usually felt without my clothes, almost as if I had taken off my skin.

Life kept to the 'even tenor' of its way. I felt a little flat with no rehearsals to attend and no lines to learn. Christmas came. Traditionally, Mother and I were alone on the Day itself, we would not have had it any other way, but on Boxing Day Moira arrived and Mother invited a couple of neighbours of ours as well. At some stage, I seem to recall, Susan Hayes dropped in with her husband to wish us the 'compliments of the season'.

Moira and I had been engaged for three years. We would have got married some time before, there was no question of our not being able to afford to marry, but a difficulty had arisen over where we should live. I think I may say in all fairness that the difficulty was entirely of Moira's making. No mother could have been more welcoming to a future daughter-in-law than mine. She actually wanted us to live with her at Simla House, she said we must think of it as our home and of her simply as our housekeeper. But Moira wanted us to buy a place of our own, so we had reached a deadlock, an impasse.

It was unfortunate that on that Boxing Day, after the others had gone, Moira brought the subject up again. Her brother (an estate agent) had told her of a bungalow for sale halfway between Simla House and her parents' home and it was what he called 'a real snip'. Fortunately, *I* thought, Mother managed to turn the conversation by telling us about the bungalow she and her parents had lived in in India, with its great colonnaded veranda, its English flower garden and its peepul tree. But Moira interrupted her.

'This is *our* future we're talking about, not your past. I thought Colin and I were getting married.'

Mother was quite alarmed. 'Aren't you? Surely Colin hasn't broken things off?'

'I suppose you don't consider the possibility *I* might break things off?'

Poor Mother could not help smiling at that. She smiled to cover her hurt. Moira could upset her very easily. For some reason this made Moira angry.

'I'm too old and unattractive to have any choice in the matter, is that what you mean?'

'Moira,' I said.

She took no notice. 'You may not realize it,'

she said, 'but marrying me will be the making of Colin. It's what he needs to make a man of him.'

It must have slipped out before Mother quite knew what she was saying. She patted Moira's knee. 'I can quite see it may be a tough assignment, dear.'

There was no quarrel. Mother would never have allowed herself to be drawn into that. But Moira became very huffy and said she wanted to go home, so I had to get the car out and take her. All the way to her parents' house I had to listen to a catalogue of her wrongs at my hands and my mother's. By the time we parted I felt dispirited and nervous, I even wondered if I was doing the right thing, contemplating matrimony in the 'sere and yellow leaf' of forty-two.

Mother had cleared the things away and gone to bed. I went into my bedroom and began undressing. Opening the wardrobe to hang up my tweed trousers, I caught sight of the wolf suit and on some impulse I put it on.

Once inside the wolf I felt calmer and, yes, happier. I sat down in an armchair but after a while I found it more comfortable to crouch, then lie stretched out, on the floor. Lying there, basking in the warmth from the gas fire on my belly and paws, I found myself remembering tales of man's affinity with wolves, Romulus and Remus suckled by a she-wolf, the ancient myth of the werewolf, abandoned children reared by wolves even in these modern times. All this seemed to deflect my mind from the discord between Moira and my mother and I was able to go to bed reasonably happily and to sleep well.

Perhaps, then, it will not seem so very strange and wonderful that the next time I felt depressed I put the suit on again. Mother was out, so I was able to have the freedom of the whole house, not just of my room. It was dusk at four but instead of putting the lights on, I prowled about the house in the twilight, sometimes catching sight of my lean grey form in the many large mirrors Mother is so fond of. Because there was so little light and our house is crammed with bulky furniture and knick-knacks, the reflection I saw looked not like a man disguised but like a real wolf that has somehow escaped and strayed into a cluttered Victorian room. Or a werewolf, that animal part of man's personality that detaches itself and wanders free while leaving behind the depleted human shape.

I crept up upon the teakwood carving of the antelope and devoured the little creature before it knew what had attacked it. I resumed my battle with the bear and we struggled in front of the fireplace, locked in a desperate hairy embrace. It was then that I heard Mother let herself in at the back door. Time had passed more quickly than I had thought. I had escaped and whisked my hind paws and tail round the bend in the stairs just before she came into the hall.

Dr Vernon-Peak seems to want to know why I began this at the age of forty-two, or rather, why I had not done it before. I wish I knew. Of course there is the simple solution that I did not have a wolf skin before, but that is not the whole answer. Was it perhaps that until then I did not know what my needs were, though partially I had satisfied them by playing the parts I was given in dramatic productions? There is one other thing. I have told him that I recall, as a very young child, having a close relationship with some large animal, a dog perhaps or a pony, though a search conducted into family history by this same assiduous Vernon-Peak has yielded no evidence that we ever kept a pet. But more of this anon.

Be that as it may, once I had lived inside the wolf, I felt the need to do so more and more. Erect on my hind legs, drawn up to my full height, I do not think I flatter myself unduly when I say I made a fine handsome animal. And having written that, I realize that I have not yet described the wolf suit, taking for granted, I suppose, that those who see this document will also see it. Yet this may not be the case. They have refused to let *me* see it, which makes me wonder if it has been cleaned and made presentable again or if it is still—but, no, there is no point in going into unsavoury details.

I have said that the body and limbs of the suit

were made of long-haired grey fur fabric. The stuff of it was coarse, hardly an attractive material for a coat, I should have thought, but very closely similar to a wolf's pelt. Mother made the paws after the fashion of fur gloves but with the padded and stiffened fingers of a pair of leather gloves for the claws. The head we bought from a jokes and games shop. It had tall prick ears, small yellow eyes and a wonderful, half-open mouth, red, voracious-looking and with a double row of white fangs. The opening for me to breathe through was just beneath the lower jaw where the head joined the powerful grey hairy throat.

As the spring came I would sometimes drive out into the countryside, park the car and slip into the skin. It was far from my ambition to be seen by anyone, though. I sought solitude. Whether I should have cared for a 'beastly' companion, that is something else again. At that time I wanted merely to wander in the woods and copses or along a hedgerow in my wolf's persona. And this I did, choosing unfrequented places, avoiding anywhere that I might come in contact with the human race. I am trying, in writing this, to explain how I felt. Principally, I felt *not human*. And to be not human is to be without human responsibilities and human cares. Inside the wolf, I laid aside with my humanity my apprehensiveness about getting married, my apprehensiveness about *not* getting married, my fear of leaving Mother on her own, my justifiable resentment at not getting the leading part in our new production. All this got left behind with the depleted sleeping man I left behind to become a happy mindless wild creature.

Our wedding had once again been postponed. The purchase of the house Moira and I had finally agreed upon fell through at the last moment. I cannot say I was altogether sorry. It was near enough to my home, in the same street in fact as Simla House, but I had begun to wonder how I would feel passing our dear old house every day yet knowing it was not under that familiar roof I should lay my head.

Moira was very upset.

Yet, 'I won't live in the same house as your mother even for three months,' she said in answer to my suggestion. 'That's a certain recipe for disaster.'

'Mother and Daddy lived with Mother's parents for twenty years,' I said.

'Yes, and look at the result.' It was then that she made that remark about my enjoying playing parts because I disliked my real self.

There was nothing more to be said except that we must keep on house-hunting.

'We can still go to Malta, I suppose,' Moira said. 'We don't have to cancel that.'

Perhaps, but it would no honeymoon. Anticipating the delights of matrimony was something I had not done up till then and had no intention of doing. And I was on my guard when Moira—Mother was out at her bridge evening—insisted on going up to my bedroom with me, ostensibly to check on the shade of the suit I had bought to get married in. She said she wanted to buy me a tie. Once there, she reclined on my bed, cajoling me to come and sit beside her.

I suppose it was because I was feeling depressed that I put on the wolf skin. I took off my jacket, but nothing more of course in front of Moira, stepped into the wolf skin, fastened it up and adjusted the head. She watched me. She had seen me in it before when she came to the pantomime.

'Why have you put that on?'

I said nothing. What could I have said? The usual contentment filled me, though, and I found myself obeying her command, loping across to the bed where she was. It seemed to come naturally to fawn on her, to rub my great prick-eared head against her breast, to enclose her hands with my paws. All kinds of fantasies filled my wolfish mind and they were of an intense piercing sweetness. If we had been on our holiday then, I do not think moral resolutions would have held me back.

But unlike the lady in The George, Moira did not take hold of my head and lay it in her lap. She jumped up and shouted at me to stop this nonsense, stop it at once, she hated it. So I did as I was told, of course I did, and got sadly out of the skin and hung it back in the cupboard. I took Moira home. On our way we called in at her brother's and looked at fresh lists of houses.

It was on one of these that we eventually settled after another month or so of picking and choosing and stalling, and we fixed our wedding for the middle of December. During the summer the company had done *Blithe Spirit* (in which I had the meagre part of Dr Bradman, Bill Harkness being Charles Condomine) and the pantomime this year was Cinderella with Susan Hayes in the name part and me as the Elder of the Ugly Sisters. I had calculated I should be back from my honeymoon just in time.

No doubt I would have been. No doubt I would have married and gone away on my honeymoon and come back to play my comic part had I not agreed to go shopping with Moira on her birthday. What happened that day changed everything.

It was a Thursday evening. The stores in the West End stay open late on Thursdays. We left our offices at five, met by arrangement and together walked up Bond Street. The last thing I had in view was that we should begin bickering again, though we had seemed to do little else lately. It started with my mentioning our honeymoon. We were outside Asprey's, walking along arm in arm. Since our house would not be ready for us to move into till the middle of January, I suggested we should go back for just two weeks to Simla House. We should be going there for Christmas in any case.

'I thought we'd decided to go to an hotel,' Moira said.

'Don't you think that's rather a waste of money?'

'I think,' she said in a grim sort of tone, 'I think it's money we daren't not spend,' and she drew her arm away from mine.

I asked her what on earth she meant.

'Once get you back there with Mummy and you'll never move.'

I treated that with the contempt it deserved and said nothing. We walked along in silence. Then Moira began talking in a low monotone, using expressions from paperback psychology which I am glad to say I have never heard from Dr Vernon-Peak. We crossed the street and entered Selfridge's. Moira was still going on about Oedipus complexes and that nonsense about making a man of me.

'Keep your voice down,' I said. 'Everyone can hear you.'

She shouted at me to shut up, she would say what she pleased. Well, she had repeatedly told me to be a man and to assert myself, so I did just that. I went up to one of the counters, wrote her a cheque for, I must admit, a good deal more than I had originally meant to give her, put it into her hands and walked off, leaving her there.

For a while I felt not displeased with myself but on the way home in the train depression set in. I should have liked to tell Mother about it but Mother would be out, playing bridge. So I had recourse to my other source of comfort, my wolf skin. The phone rang several times while I was gambolling about the rooms but I did not answer it. I knew it was Moira. I was on the floor with Grandfather's stuffed eagle in my paws and my teeth in its neck when Mother walked in.

Bridge had ended early. One of the ladies had been taken ill and rushed to hospital. I had been too intent on my task to see the light come on or hear the door. She stood there in her old fur coat, looking at me. I let the eagle fall, I bowed my head, I wanted to die I was so ashamed and embarrassed. How little I really knew my mother! My dear faithful companion, my only friend! Might I not say, my other self?

She smiled. I could hardly believe it but she was smiling. It was that wonderful, conspiratorial, rather naughty smile of hers. 'Hallo,' she said. 'Are you going all loopy?'

In a moment she was down on her knees beside me, the fur coat enveloping her, and together we worried at the eagle, engaged in battle with the bear, attacked the antelope. Together we bounded into the hall to pounce upon the sleeping tigers. Mother kept laughing (and growling too) saying, what a relief, what a relief! I think we embraced. Next day when I got home she was waiting for me, transformed and ready. She had made herself an animal suit, she must have worked on it all day, out of the snow leopard skin and a length of white fur fabric. I could see her eyes dancing through the gap in its throat.

'You don't know how I've longed to be an animal again,' she said. 'I used to be animals when you were a baby, I was a dog for a long time and then I was a bear, but your father found out and he didn't like it. I had to stop.'

So that was what I dimly remembered. I said she looked like the Queen of the Beasts.

'Do I, Loopy?' she said.

We had a wonderful weekend, Mother and I. Wolf and leopard, we breakfasted together that morning. Then we played. We played all over the house, sometimes fighting, sometimes dancing, hunting of course, carrying off our prey to the lairs we made for ourselves among the furniture. We went out in the car, drove into the country and there in a wood got into our skins and for many happy hours roamed wild among the trees.

There seemed no reason, during those two days, to become human again at all, but on the Tuesday I had a rehearsal, on the Monday morning I had to go off to work. It was coming down to earth, back to what we call reality, with a nasty bang. Still, it had its amusing side too. A lady in the train trod on my toe and I had growled at her before I remembered and turned it into a cough.

All through that weekend neither of us had bothered to answer the phone. In the office I had no choice and it was there that Moira caught me. Marriage had come to seem remote, something grotesque, something that others did, not me. Animals do not marry. But that was not the sort of thing I could say to Moira. I promised to ring her, I said we must meet before the week was out.

I suppose she did tell me she would come over on the Thursday evening and show me what she had bought with the money I had given her. She knew Mother was always out on Thursdays. I suppose Moira did tell me and I failed to take it in. Nothing was important to me but being animals with Mother, Loopy and the Queen of the Beasts.

Each night as soon as I got home we made ourselves ready for our evening's games. How harmless it all was! How innocent! Like the gentle creatures in the dawn of the world before man came. Like the Garden of Eden after Adam and Eve had been sent away.

The lady who had been taken ill at the bridge evening had since died, so this week it was cancelled. But would Mother have gone anyway? Probably not. Our animal capers meant as much to her as they did to me, almost more perhaps, for she had denied herself so long. We were sitting at the dining table, eating our evening meal. Mother had cooked, I recall, a rack of lamb so that we might later gnaw the bones. We never ate it, of course, and I have since wondered what became of it. But we did begin our soup. The bread was at my end of the table, with the bread board and the long sharp knife.

Moira, when she called and I was alone, was in the habit of letting herself in by the back door. We did not hear her, neither of us heard her, though I do remember Mother's noble head lifted a fraction before Moira came in, her fangs bared and her ears pricked. Moira opened the dining-room door and walked in. I can see her now, the complacent smile on her lips fading and the scream starting to come. She was wearing what must have been my present, a full-length white sheepskin coat.

And then? This is what Dr Vernon-Peak will particularly wish to know but what I cannot clearly remember. I remember that as the door opened I was holding the bread knife in my paws. I think I remember letting out a low growl and poising myself to spring. But what came after?

The last things I can recall before they brought me here are the blood on my fur and the two wild predatory creatures crouched on the floor over the body of the lamb.

FEN HALL

When children paint a picture of a tree they always do the trunk brown. But trees seldom have brown trunks. Birches are silver, beeches pewter colour, planes grey and yellow, walnuts black and the bark of oaks, chestnuts and sycamores green with lichen. Pringle had never noticed any of this until he came to Fen Hall. After that, once his eyes had been opened and he had seen what things were really like, he would have painted trees with bark in different colours but next term he stopped doing art. It was just as well, he had never been very good at it, and perhaps by then he wouldn't have felt like painting trees anyway. Or even looking at them much.

Mr Liddon met them at the station in an old Volvo estate car. They were loaded down with camping gear, the tent and sleeping bags and cooking pots and a Calor gas burner in case it was too windy to keep a fire going. It had been very windy lately, the summer cool and sunless. Mr Liddon was Pringle's father's friend and Pringle had met him once before, years ago when he was a little kid, but still it was up to him to introduce the others. He spoke with wary politeness.

'This is John and this is Roger. They're

brothers.'

Pringle didn't say anything about Roger always being called Hodge. He sensed that Mr Liddon wouldn't call him Hodge any more than he would call *him* Pringle. He was right.

'Parents well, are they, Peregrine?'

Pringle said yes. He could see a gleam in John's eye that augured teasing to come. Hodge, who was always thinking of his stomach, said:

'Could we stop on the way, Mr Liddon, and buy some food?'

Mr Liddon cast up his eyes. Pringle could tell he was going to be 'one of those' grown-ups. They all got into the car with their stuff and a mile or so out of town Mr Liddon stopped at a self-service shop. He didn't go inside with them which was just as well. He would only have called what they bought junk food.

Fen Hall turned out to be about seven miles away. They went through a village called Fedgford and a little way beyond it turned down a lane that passed through a wood.

'That's where you'll have your camp,' Mr Liddon said.

Of necessity, because the lane was no more than a rough track, he was driving slowly. He pointed in among the trees. The wood had a mysterious look as if full of secrets. In the aisles between the trees the light was greenish-gold and misty. There was a muted twittering of birds and a cooing of doves. Pringle began to feel excited. It was nicer than he had expected. A little further on the wood petered out into a plantation of tall straight trees with green trunks growing in rows, thc ground between them all overgrown with a spiky plant that had a curious prehistoric look to it.

'Those trees are poplars,' Mr Liddon said. You could tell he was a schoolteacher. 'They're grown as a crop.'

This was a novel idea to Pringle. 'What sort of a crop?'

'Twenty-five years after they're planted they're cut down and used for making matchsticks. If they don't fall down first. We had a couple go over in the gales last winter.'

Pringle wasn't listening. He had seen the house. It was like a house in a dream, he thought, though he didn't quite know what he meant by that. Houses he saw in actual dreams were much like his own home or John and Hodge's, suburban Surrey semidetached. This house, when all the trees were left behind and no twig or leaf or festoon of wild clematis obscured it, stood basking in the sunshine with the confidence of something alive, as if secure in its own perfection. Dark mulberry colour, of small Tudor bricks, it had a roof of many irregular planes and gables and a cluster of chimneys like candles. The windows with the sun on them were plates of gold between the mullions. Under the eaves swallows had built their lumpy sagging nests.

'Leave your stuff in the car. I'll be taking you back up to the wood in ten minutes. Just thought you'd like to get your bearings, see where everything is first. There's the outside tap over there which you'll use of course. And you'll find a shovel and an axe in there which I rely on you to replace.'

It was going to be the biggest house Pringle had ever set foot in—not counting places like Hampton Court and Woburn. Fen Hall. It looked and the name sounded like a house in a book, not real at all. The front door was of oak, studded with iron and set back under a porch that was dark and carved with roses. Mr Liddon took them in the back way. He took them into a kitchen that was exactly Pringle's idea of the lowest sort of slum.

He was shocked. At first he couldn't see much because it had been bright outside but he could smell something dank and frowsty. When his vision adjusted he found they were in a huge room or cavern with two small windows and about four hundred square feet of squalor between them. Islanded were a small white electric oven and a small white fridge. The floor was of brick, very uneven, the walls of irregular green-painted peeling plaster with a bubbly kind of growth coming through it. Stacks of dirty dishes filled a stone sink of the kind his mother had bought at a sale and made a cactus garden in. The whole place was grossly untidy with piles of washing lying about. John and Hodge, having taken it all in, were standing there with blank faces and shifting eyes.

Mr Liddon's manner had changed slightly. He no longer kept up the hectoring tone. While explaining to them that this was where they must come if they needed anything, to the back door, he began a kind of ineffectual tidying up, cramming things into the old wooden cupboards, sweeping crumbs off the table and dropping them into the sink. John said:

'Is is all right for us to have a fire?'

'So long as you're careful. Not if the wind gets up again. I don't have to tell you where the wood is, you'll find it lying about.' Mr Liddon opened a door and called, 'Flora!'

A stone-flagged passage could be seen beyond. No one came. Pringle knew Mr Liddon had a wife, though no children. His parents had told him that Mr and Mrs Liddon had bought a marvellous house in the country a year before and he and a couple of his friends could go and camp in the grounds if they wanted to. Further information he had picked up when they didn't know he was listening. Tony Liddon hadn't had two halfpennies to rub together until his aunt died and left him a bit of money. It couldn't have been much surely. Anyway he had spent it all on Fen Hall, he had always wanted an old place like that. The upkeep was going to be a drain on him and goodness knows how he would manage.

Pringle hadn't been much interested in all this. Now it came back to him. Mr Liddon and his father had been at university together but Mr Liddon hadn't a wife then. Pringle had never met the wife and nor had his parents. Anyway it was clear they were not to wait for her. They got back into the car and went to find a suitable camping site.

It was a relief when Mr Liddon went away and left them to it. The obvious place to camp was on the high ground in a clearing and to make their fire in a hollow Mr Liddon said was probably a disused gravel pit. The sun was low, making long shafts of light that pierced the groves of birch and crab apple. Mistletoe hung in the oak trees like green bird's nests. It was warm and murmurous with flies. John was adept at putting up the tent and gave them orders.

'Peregrine,' he said. 'Like a sort of mad bird.'

Hodge capered about, his thumbs in his ears and his hands flapping. 'Tweet, tweet, mad bird. His master chains him up like a dog. Tweet, tweet, birdie!'

'I'd rather be a hunting falcon than Roger the lodger the sod,' said Pringle and he shoved Hodge and they both fell over and rolled about grappling on the ground until John kicked them and told them to stop it and give a hand, he couldn't do the lot on his own.

It was good in the camp that night, not windy but still and mild after the bad summer they'd had. They made a fire and cooked tomato soup and fish fingers and ate a whole packet of the biscuits called iced bears. They were in their bags in the tent, John reading the *Observer's Book of Common Insects*, Pringle a thriller set in a Japanese prison camp his parents would have taken away if they'd known about it, and Hodge listening to his radio, when Mr Liddon came up with a torch to check on them.

'Just to see if you're OK. Everything shipshape and Bristol fashion?'

Pringle thought that an odd thing to say considering the mess in his own house. Mr Liddon made a fuss about the candles they had lit and they promised to put them out, though of course they didn't. It was very silent in the night up there in the wood, the deepest silence Pringle had ever known, a quiet that was somehow heavy as if a great dark beast had laid down on the wood and quelled every sound beneath under its dense soft fur. He didn't think of this for very long because he was asleep two minutes after they blew the candles out.

Next morning the weather wasn't so nice. It was dull and cool for August. John saw a Brimstone butterfly which pleased him because the species was getting rarer. They all walked into Fedgford and bought sausages and then found they hadn't a frying pan. Pringle went down to the house on his own to see if he could borrow one.

Unlike most men Mr Liddon would be at home because of the school holidays. Pringle expected to see him working in the garden which even he could see was a mess. But he wasn't anywhere about. Pringle banged on the back door with his fist—there was neither bell nor knocker—but no one came. The door wasn't locked. He wondered if it would be all right to go in and then he went in.

The mess in the kitchen was rather worse. A large white and tabby cat was on the table eating something it probably shouldn't have been eating out of a paper bag. Pringle had a curious feeling that it would somehow be quite permissible for him to go on into the house. Something told him—though it was not a something based on observation or even guesswork—that Mr Liddon wasn't in. He went into the passage he had seen the day before through the open door. This led into a large stone-flagged hall. The place was dark with heavy dark beams going up the walls and across the ceilings and it was cold. It smelled of damp. The smell was like mushrooms that have been left in a paper bag at the back of the fridge and forgotten. Pringle pushed open a likely looking door, some instinct making him give a warning cough.

The room was enormous, its ceiling all carved beams and cobwebs. Even Pringle could see that the few small bits of furniture in it would have been more suitable for the living room of a bungalow. A woman was standing by the tall, diamond-paned, mullioned window, holding something blue and sparkling up to the light. She was strangely dressed in a long skirt, her hair falling loosely down her back, and she stood so still, gazing at the blue object with both arms raised, that for a moment Pringle had an uneasy feeling she wasn't a woman at all but the ghost of a woman. Then she turned round and smiled.

'Hallo,' she said. 'Are you one of our campers?'

She was at least as old as Mr Liddon but her hair hung down like one of the girls' at school. Her face was pale and not pretty yet when she smiled it was a wonderful face. Pringle registered that, staring at her. It was a face of radiant kind sensitivity, though it was to be some years before he could express what he had felt in those terms.

'I'm Pringle,' he said, and because he sensed that she would understand, 'I'm called Peregrine really but I get people to call me Pringle.'

'I don't blame you. I'd do the same in your place.' She had a quiet unaffected voice. 'I'm Flora Liddon. You call me Flora.'

He didn't think he could do that and knew he

would end up calling her nothing. 'I came to see if I could borrow a frying pan.'

'Of course you can.' She added, 'If I can find one.' She held the thing in her hand out to him and he saw it was a small glass bottle. 'Do you think it's pretty?'

He looked at it doubtfully. It was just a bottle. On the window sill behind her were more bottles, mostly of clear colourless glass but among them dark green ones with fluted sides.

'There are wonderful things to be found here. You can dig and find rubbish heaps that go back to Elizabethan times. And there was a Roman settlement down by the river. Would you like to see a Roman coin?'

It was black, misshapen, lumpy, with an ugly man's head on it. She showed him a jar of thick bubbly green glass and said it was the best piece of glass she'd found to date. They went out to the kitchen. Finding a frying pan wasn't easy but talking to her was. By the time she had washed up a pan which she had found full of congealed fat he had told her all about the camp and their walk to Fedgford and what the butcher had said:

'I hope you're going to wash yourselves before you cook my nice clean sausages.'

And she told him what a lot needed doing to the house and grounds and how they'd have to do it all themselves because they hadn't much money. She wasn't any good at painting or sewing or gardening or even housework, come to that. Pottering about and looking at things was what she liked.

'"What is this life if, full of care, we have no time to stand and stare?"'

He knew where that came from. W. H. Davies, the Super-tramp. They had done it at school.

'I'd have been a good tramp,' she said. 'It would have suited me.'

The smile irradiated her plain face.

They cooked the sausages for lunch and went on an insect-hunting expedition with John. The dragonflies he had promised them down by the river were not to be seen but he found what he said was a caddis, though it looked like a bit of twig to Pringle. Hodge ate five Mars bars during the course of the afternoon. They came upon the white and tabby cat with a mouse in its jaws. Undeterred by an audience, it bit the mouse in two and the tiny heart rolled out. Hodge said faintly, 'I think I'm going to be sick,' and was. They still resolved to have a cat-watch on the morrow and see how many mice it caught in a day.

By that time the weather was better. The sun didn't shine but it had got warmer again. They found the cat in the poplar plantation, stalking something among the prehistoric weeds John said were called horse tails. The poplars had trunks almost as green as grass and their leafy tops, very high up there in the pale blue sky, made rustling whispering sounds in the breeze. That was when Pringle noticed about tree trunks not being brown. The trunks of the Scotch pines were a clear pinkish-red, as bright as flowers when for a moment the sun shone. He pointed this out to the others but they didn't seem interested.

'You sound like our auntie,' said Hodge. 'She does flower arrangements for the church.'

'And throws up when she sees a bit of blood, I expect,' said Pringle. 'It runs in your family.'

Hodge lunged at him and he tipped Hodge up and they rolled about wrestling among the horse tails. By four in the afternoon the cat had caught six mice. Flora came out and told them the cat's name was Tabby which obscurely pleased Pringle. If she had said Snowflake or Persephone or some other daft name people called animals he would have felt differently about her, though he couldn't possibly have said why. He wouldn't have liked her so much.

A man turned up in a Land-Rover as they were making their way back to camp. He said he had been to the house and knocked but no one seemed to be at home. Would they give Mr or Mrs Liddon a message from him? His name was Porter, Michael Porter, and he was an archaeologist in an amateur sort of way, Mr Liddon knew all about it, and they were digging in the lower meadow and they'd come on a dump of nineteenth-century stuff. He was going to dig deeper, uncover the next layer, so if Mrs Liddon was interested in the top, now was her chance to have a look.

'Can we as well?' said Pringle.

Porter said they were welcome. No one would be working there next day. He had just heard the weather forecast on his car radio and gale-force winds were promised. Was that their camp up there? Make sure the tent was well anchored down, he said, and he drove off up the lane.

Pringle checked the tent. It seemed firm enough. They got into it and fastened the flap but they were afraid to light the candles and had John's storm lantern on instead. The wood was silent no longer. The wind made loud sirenlike howls and a rushing rending sound like canvas being torn. When that happened the tent flapped and bellied like a sail on a ship at sea. Sometimes the wind stopped altogether and there were a few seconds of silence and calm. Then it came back with a rush and a roar. John was reading Frohawk's *Complete Book of British Butterflies*, Pringle the Japanese prison-camp thriller and Hodge was trying to listen to his radio. But it wasn't much use and after a while they put the lantern out and lay in the dark.

About five minutes afterwards there came the strongest gust of wind so far, one of the canvas-tearing gusts but ten times fiercer than the last; and then, from the south of them, down towards the house, a tremendous rending crash.

John said, 'I think we'll have to do something.' His voice was brisk but it wasn't quite steady and Pringle knew he was as scared as they were. 'We'll have to get out of here.'

Pringle put the lantern on again. It was just ten.

'The tent's going to lift off,' said Hodge.

Crawling out of his sleeping bag, Pringle was wondering what they ought to do, if it would be all right, or awful, to go down to the house, when the tent flap was pulled open and Mr Liddon put his head in. He looked cross.

'Come on, the lot of you. You can't stay here. Bring your sleeping bags and we'll find you somewhere in the house for the night.'

A note in his voice made it sound as if the storm were their fault. Pringle found his shoes, stuck his feet into them and rolled up his sleeping bag. John carried the lantern. Mr Liddon shone his own torch to light their way. In the wood there was shelter but none in the lane and the wind buffeted them as they walked. It was all noise, you couldn't see much, but as they passed the plantation Mr Liddon swung the light up and Pringle saw what had made the crash. One of the poplars had gone over and was lying on its side with its roots in the air.

For some reason—perhaps because it was just about on this spot that they had met Michael Porter—John remembered the message. Mr

Liddon said OK and thanks. They went into the house through the back door. A tile blew off the roof and crashed on to the path just as the door closed behind them.

There were beds up in the bedrooms but without blankets or sheets on them and the mattresses were damp. Pringle thought them spooky bedrooms, dirty and draped with spiders' webs, and he wasn't sorry they weren't going to sleep there. There was the same smell of old mushrooms and a smell of paint as well where Mr Liddon had started work on a ceiling.

At the end of the passage, looking out of a window, Flora stood in a nightgown with a shawl over it. Pringle, who sometimes read ghost stories, saw her as the Grey Lady of Fen Hall. She was in the dark, the better to see the forked lightning that had begun to leap on the horizon beyond the river.

'I love to watch a storm,' she said, turning and smiling at them.

Mr Liddon had snapped a light on. 'Where are these boys to sleep?'

It was as if it didn't concern her. She wasn't unkind but she wasn't involved either. 'Oh, in the drawing room, I should think.'

'We have seven bedrooms.'

Flora said no more. A long roll of thunder shook the house. Mr Liddon took them downstairs and through the drawing room into a sort of study where they helped him make up beds of cushions on the floor. The wind howled round the house and Pringle heard another tile go. He lay in the dark, listening to the storm. The others were asleep, he could tell by their steady breathing. Inside the bag it was quite warm and he felt snug and safe. After a while he heard Mr Liddon and Flora quarrelling on the other side of the door.

Pringle's parents quarrelled a lot and he hated it, it was the worst thing in the world, though less bad now than when he was younger. He could only just hear Mr Liddon and Flora and only disjointed words, abusive and angry on the man's part, indifferent, amused on the woman's, until one sentence rang out clearly. Her voice was penetrating though it was so quiet:

'We want such different things!'

He wished they would stop. And suddenly they did, with the coming of the rain. The rain came, exploded rather, crashing at the windows and on the old sagging depleted roof. It was strange that a sound like that, a loud constant roar, could send you to sleep . . .

She was in the kitchen when he went out there in the morning. John and Hodge slept on, in spite of the bright watery sunshine that streamed through the dirty diamond window panes. A clean world outside, new-washed. Indoors the same chaos, the kitchen with the same smell of fungus and dirty dishcloths, though the windows were open. Flora sat at the table on which sprawled a welter of plates, indefinable garments, bits of bread and fruit rinds, an open can of cat food. She was drinking coffee and Tabby lay on her lap.

'There's plenty in the pot if you want some.'

She was the first grown-up in whose house he had stayed who didn't ask him how he had slept. Nor was she going to cook breakfast for him. She told him where the eggs were and bread and butter. Pringle remembered he still hadn't returned her frying pan which might be the only one she had.

He made himself a pile of toast and found a jar of marmalade. The grass and the paths, he could see through an open window, were littered with broken bits of twig and leaf. A cock pheasant strutted across the shaggy lawn.

'Did the storm damage a lot of things?' he asked.

'I don't know. Tony got up early to look. There may be more poplars down.'

Pringle ate his toast. The cat had begun to purr in an irregular throbbing way. Her hand kneaded its ears and neck. She spoke, but not perhaps to Pringle or the cat, or for them if they cared to hear.

'So many people are like that. The whole of life is a preparation for life, not living.'

Pringle didn't know what to say. He said nothing. She got up and walked away, still carrying the cat, and then after a while he heard music coming faintly from a distant part of the house.

There were two poplars down in the plantation and each had left a crater four or five feet deep. As they went up the lane to check on their camp, Pringle and John and Hodge had a good look at them, their green trunks laid low, their tangled roots in the air. Apart from everything having got a bit blown about up at the camp and the stuff they had left out soaked through, there was no real damage done. The wood itself had afforded protection to their tent.

It seemed a good time to return the frying pan. After that they would have to walk to Fedgford for some sausages—unless one of the Liddons offered a lift. It was with an eye to this, Pringle had to admit, that he was taking the pan back.

But Mr Liddon, never one to waste time, was already at work in the plantation. He had lugged a chain saw up there and was preparing to cut up the poplars where they lay. When he saw them in the lane he came over.

'How did you sleep?'

Pringle said, 'OK, thanks,' but Hodge, who had been very resentful about not being given a hot drink or something to eat, muttered that he had been too hungry to sleep. Mr Liddon took no notice. He seemed jumpy and nervous. He said to Pringle that if they were going to the house would they tell Mrs Liddon—he never called her Flora to them—that there was what looked like a dump of Victorian glass in the crater where the bigger poplar had stood.

'They must have planted the trees over the top without knowing.'

Pringle looked into the crater and sure enough he could see bits of coloured glass and a bottleneck and a jug or tankard handle protruding from the tumbled soil. He left the others there, fascinated by the chain saw, and went to take the frying pan back. Flora was in the drawing room, playing records of tinkly piano music. She jumped up, quite excited, when he told her about the bottle dump.

They walked back to the plantation together, Tabby following, walking a little way behind them like a dog. Pringle knew he hadn't a hope of getting that lift now. Mr Liddon had already got the crown of the big poplar sawn off. In the short time since the storm its pale silvery-green leaves had begun to wither. John asked if they could have a go with the chain saw but Mr Liddon said not likely, did they think he was crazy? And if they wanted to get to the butcher before the shop closed for lunch they had better get going now.

Flora, her long skirt hitched up, had clambered down into the crater. If she had stood up in it her head and shoulders, perhaps all of her from the waist up, would have come above its rim, for poplars have shallow roots. But she didn't stand up. She squatted down, using her trowel, extracting small glass objects from the leafmould. The chain saw whined, slicing through the top of the poplar trunk. Pringle, watching with the others, had a feeling something was wrong about the way Mr Liddon was doing it. He didn't know what though. He could only think of a funny film he had once seen in which a man, sitting on a branch, sawed away at the bit between him and the tree trunk, necessarily falling off himself when the branch fell. But Mr Liddon wasn't sitting on anything. He was just sawing up a fallen tree from the crown to the bole. The saw sliced through again, making four short logs now as well as the bole.

'Cut along now, you boys,' he said. 'You don't want to waste the day mooning about here.'

Flora looked up and winked at Pringle. It wasn't unkind, just conspiratorial, and she smiled too, holding up a small glowing red glass bottle for him to see. He and John and Hodge moved slowly off, reluctantly, dawdling because the walk ahead would be boring and long. Through the horse tails, up the bank, looking back when the saw whined again.

But Pringle wasn't actually looking when it happened. None of them was. They had had their final look and had begun to trudge up the lane. The sound made them turn, a kind of swishing lurch and then a heavy plopping, sickening, dull crash. They cried out, all three of them, but no one else did, not Flora or Mr Liddon. Neither of them made a sound.

Mr Liddon was standing with his arms held out, his mouth open and his eyes staring. The pile of logs lay beside him but the tree trunk was gone, sprung back roots and all when the last cut went through, tipped the balance and made its base heavier than its top. Pringle put his hand over his mouth and held it there. Hodge, who was nothing more than a fat baby really, had begun to cry. Fearfully, slowly, they converged, all four of them, on the now upright tree under whose roots she lay.

The police came and a farmer and his son and some men from round about. Between them they got the tree over on its side again but by then Flora was dead. Perhaps she died as soon as the bole and the mass of roots hit her. Pringle wasn't there to see. Mr Liddon had put the plantation out of bounds and said they were to stay in camp until someone came to drive them to the station. It was Michael Porter who turned up in the late afternoon and checked they'd got everything packed up and the camp site tidied. He told them Flora was dead. They got to the station in his Land-Rover in time to catch the five-fifteen for London.

On the way to the station he didn't mention the bottle dump he had told them about. Pringle wondered if Mr Liddon had ever said anything to Flora about it. All the way home in the train he kept thinking of something odd. The first time he went up the lane to the camp that morning he was sure there hadn't been any glass in the tree crater. He would have seen the gleam of it and he hadn't. He didn't say anything to John and Hodge, though. What would have been the point?

Three years afterwards Pringle's parents got an invitation to Mr Liddon's wedding. He was marrying the daughter of a wealthy local builder and the reception was to be at Fen Hall, the house in the wood. Pringle didn't go, being too old now to tag about after his parents. He had gone off trees anyway.

FATHER'S DAY

Teddy had once read in a story written by a Victorian that a certain character liked 'to have things pleasant about him'. The phrase had stuck in his mind. He too liked to have things pleasant about him.

It was hoped that pleasantness would prevail while they were all away on holiday together. Teddy was beginning to be afraid they might get on each other's nerves. Anyway, it would be the last time for years the four of them would be able to go away in October for both Emma and Andrew started school in the spring.

'A pity,' Anne said, 'because May and October are absolutely the best times in the Greek Islands.'

She and Teddy had bought the house with the money Teddy's mother had left him. The previous year they had been there twice and again last May. They hadn't been able to go out in the evenings because they had no baby-sitter. Having Michael and Linda there would make it possible for each couple to go out every other night.

'If Michael will trust us with his children,' said Teddy.

'He isn't as bad as that.'

'I didn't say he was bad. He's my brother-in-law and I've got to put up with him. He's all right. It's just that he's so nuts about his kids I sometimes wonder how he dares leave them with their own mother when he goes to work.'

He was recalling the time they had all spent at Chichester in July and how the evening had been spoilt by Michael's insisting on phoning the baby-sitter before the play began, during the interval and before they began the drive home. And when he wasn't on the phone or obliged to be silent in the theatre he had talked continually about Andrew and Alison in a fretful way.

'He's under a lot of stress,' Linda had whispered to her sister. 'He's going through a bad patch at work.'

Teddy didn't think it natural for a man to be so involved with his children. He was fond of his own children, of course he was, and anxious enough about them when he had cause, but they were little still and, let's face it, sometimes tiresome and boring. He looked forward to the time when they were older and there could be real companionship. Michael was more like a mother than a father, a mother hen. Teddy, for his sins, had occasionally changed napkins and made up feeds but Michael actually seemed to enjoy doing these things and talking about them afterwards. Teddy hoped he wouldn't be treated to too much Dr Jolly philosophy while on Stamnos.

Just before they went, about a week before,

Valerie Wilton's marriage broke up. Valerie had been at school with Anne, though just as much Linda's friend, and had written long letters to both of them, explaining everything and asking for their understanding. She had gone off with a man she met at her Commercial French evening class. Apparently the affair had been going on for a long time but Valerie's husband had known nothing about it and her departure had come to him as a total shock. He came round and poured out his troubles to Anne and drank a lot of scotch and broke down and cried. For all Teddy knew, he did the same at Linda's. Teddy stayed out of it, he didn't want to get involved. Liking to have things pleasant about him, he declined gently but firmly even to discuss it with Anne.

'Linda says it's really upset Michael,' said Anne. 'He identifies with George, you see. He's so emotional.'

'I said I wasn't going to talk about it, darling, and by golly I'm not!'

During the flight Michael had Alison on his lap and Andrew in the seat beside him. Anne remarked in a plaintive way that it was all right for Linda. Teddy saw that Linda slept most of the way. She was a beautiful girl—better-looking than Anne, most people thought, though Teddy didn't—and now that Michael was making more money had bought a lot of new clothes and was having her hair cut in a very stylish way. Teddy, who was quite observant, especially of attractive things, noted that recently she had stopped wearing trousers. He looked appreciatively across the aisle at her long slim legs.

They changed planes at Athens. It was a fine clear day and as the aircraft came in to land you could see the wine jar shape of the island from which it took its name. Stamnos was no more than twenty miles long but the road was poor and rutted, winding up and down over low olive-clad mountains, and it took over an hour for the car to get to Votani at the wine jar's mouth. The driver, a Stamniot, was one of those Greeks who spend their youth in Australia before returning home to start a business on the money they have made. He talked all the way in a harsh clattering Greek-Strine while his radio played bouzouki music and Alison whimpered in Michael's arms. It was hot for the time of year.

Tim, who was a bad traveller, had been carsick twice by the time they reached Votani. The car couldn't go up the narrow flagged street, so they had to get out and carry the baggage, the driver helping with a case in each hand and one on his head. Michael didn't carry a case because he had Andrew on his shoulders and Alison in his arms.

The houses of Votani covered a shallow conical hill so that it looked from a distance like a heap of pastel-coloured pebbles. Close to, the buildings were neat, crowded, interlocking, hung with jasmine and bougainvillea, and the hill itself was surmounted by the ruins, extravagantly picturesque, of a Crusaders' fortress. Teddy and Anne's house was three fishermen's cottages that its previous owner had converted into one. It had a lot of little staircases on account of being built on the steep hillside. From the bedroom where the four children would sleep you could see the eastern walls of the fortress, a dark blue expanse of sea, and smudgy on the horizon, the Turkish coast. The dark came quickly after the sun had gone. Teddy, when abroad, always found that disconcerting after England with its long protracted dusks.

Within an hour of reaching Votani he found himself walking down the main street—a stone-walled defile smelling of jasmine and lit by lamps on iron brackets—towards Agamemnon's Bar. He felt guilty about going out and leaving Anne to put the children to bed. But it had been Anne's suggestion, indeed Anne's insistence, that he should take Michael out for a drink before supper. A whispered colloquy had established they both thought Michael looked 'washed out' (Anne's expression) and 'fed up' (Teddy's) and no wonder, the way he had been attending to Andrew's and Alison's wants all day.

Michael had needed a lot of persuading, had at first been determined to stay and help Linda, and it therefore rather surprised Teddy when he began on a grumbling tirade against women's liberation.

'I sometimes wonder what they mean, they're not "equal",' he said. 'They have the children, don't they? We can't do that. I consider that makes them *superior* rather than inferior.'

'I know I shouldn't like to have a baby,' said Teddy irrelevantly.

'It's because of that,' said Michael as if Teddy hadn't spoken, 'that we need to master them. We have to for our own sakes. Where should we be if they had the babies and the whip hand too?'

Teddy said vaguely that he didn't know about whip hand but someone had said that the hand which rocks the cradle rules the world. By this time they were in Agamemnon's, sitting at a table on the vine-covered terrace. The other customers were all Stamniots, some of whom recognized Teddy and nodded at him and smiled. Most of the tourists had gone by now and all but one of the hotels were closed for the winter. Hedonistic Teddy, wanting to have things pleasant about him, hadn't cared for the turn the conversation was taking. He began telling Michael how amused he and Anne had been when they found that the proprietor of the bar was called after the great hero of classical antiquity and how ironical it had seemed, for this Agamemnon was small and fat. Here he was forced to break off as stout smiling Agamemnon came to take their order.

Michael had no intention of letting him begin once more on the subject of Stamniot names. He spoke in a rapid violent tone, his thin dark face pinched with intensity.

'A man can lose his children any time and through no fault of his own. Have you ever thought of that?'

Teddy looked at him. Notions of kidnapping, of mortal illness, came into his head. 'What do you mean?'

'It could happen to you or me, to any of us. A man can lose his children overnight and he can't do a thing about it. He may be a good faithful husband, a good provider, a devoted father—that won't make a scrap of difference. Look at George Wilton. What did George do wrong? Nothing. But he lost his children just the same. One day they were living with him in his house and the next they were in Gerrards Cross with Valerie and that Commercial French chap and he'll be lucky if he sees them once a fortnight.'

'I see what you're getting at,' said Teddy. 'He couldn't look after them though, could he? He's got to go to work. I mean, I see it's unfair, but you can't take kids away from their mother, can you?'

'Apparently not. But you can take them from

their father.'

'I shouldn't worry about one isolated case if I were you,' said Teddy, feeling very uncomfortable. 'You want to forget that sort of thing while you're here. Unwind a bit.'

'An isolated case is just what it isn't. There's someone at work, John Frost, you don't know him. He and his wife split up—at her wish, naturally—and she took their baby with her as a matter of course. And George told me the same thing happened in his brother's marriage a couple of years back. Three children he had, he lived for his children, and now he gets to take them to the zoo every other Saturday.'

'Maybe,' said Teddy who had his moments of shrewdness, 'if he'd lived for his wife a bit more it wouldn't have happened.'

He was glad to be back in the house. In bed that night he told Anne about it. Anne said Michael was an obsessional person. When he'd first met Linda he'd been obsessed by her and now it was Andrew and Alison. He wasn't very nice to Linda these days, she'd noticed, he was always watching her in an unpleasant way. And when Linda had suggested she take the children up to the fortress in the morning if he wanted to go down to the harbour and see the fishing boats come in, he had said:

'No way am I going to allow you up there on your own with my children.'

Later in the week they all went. You had to

keep your eye on the children every minute of the time, there were so many places to fall over, fissures in the walls, crumbling corners, holes that opened on to the empty blue air. But the view from the eastern walls, breached in a dozen places, where the crag fell away in an almost vertical sweep to a beach of creamy-silver sand and brown rocks, was the best on Stamnos. You could see the full extent of the bay that was the lip of the wine jar and the sea with its scattering of islands and the low mountains of Turkey behind which, Teddy thought romantically, perhaps lay the Plain of Troy. The turf up here was slippery, dry as clean combed hair. No rain had fallen on Stamnos for five months. The sky was a smooth mauvish-blue, cloudless and clear. Emma and Andrew, the bigger ones, ran about on the slippery turf, enjoying it because it was slippery, falling over and slithering down the slopes.

Teddy had successfully avoided being alone with Michael since their conversation in the bar but later that day Michael caught him. He put it that way to himself but in fact it was more as if, unwittingly, he had caught Michael. He had gone down to the grocery store, had bought the red apples, the feta cheese and the olive oil Anne wanted, and had passed into the inner room which was a secondhand bookstore and stuffed full with paperbacks in a variety of European languages discarded by the thousand tourists who had come to Votani that summer. The room was empty but for Michael who was standing in a far corner, having taken down from a shelf a novel whose title was its heroine's name.

'That's a Swedish translation,' said Teddy gently.

'Oh, is it? Yes, I see.'

'The English books are all over here.'

Michael's face looked haggard in the gloom of the shop. He didn't tan easily in spite of being so dark. They came out into the sunlight, Teddy carrying his purchases in the string bag, pausing now and then to look down over a wall or through a gateway. Down there the meadows spread out to the sea, olives with the black nets laid under them to catch the harvest, cypresses thin as thorns. The shepherd's dog was bringing the flock in and the sheep bells made a distant tinkling music. Michael's shadow fell across the sunlit wall.

'I was off in a dream,' said Teddy. 'Beautiful, isn't it? I love it. It makes me quite sad to think we shan't come here in October again for maybe—what? Twelve or fourteen years?'

'I can't say it bothers me to have to make sacrifices for the sake of my children.'

Teddy thought this reproof uncalled for and he would have liked to rejoin with something sharp. But he wasn't very good at innuendo. And in any case before he could come up with anything Michael had begun on quite a different subject.

'The law in Greece has relaxed a lot in the past few years in favour of women—property rights and divorce and so on.'

Teddy said, not without a spark of malice, 'Jolly good, isn't it?'

'Those things are the first cracks in the fabric of a society that lead to its ultimate breakdown.'

'*Our* society hasn't broken down.'

Michael gave a scathing laugh as if at the naivety of this comment. 'Throughout the nineteenth century,' he said in severe lecturing tones, 'and a good deal of this one, if a woman left her husband the children stayed with him as a matter of course. The children were never permitted to be with the guilty party. And there was a time, not so long ago, when a man could use the law to compel his wife to return to him.'

'You wouldn't want that back, would you?'

'I'll tell you something, Teddy. There's a time coming when children won't have fathers—that is, it won't matter who your father is any more. You'll know your mother and that'll be enough. That's the way things are moving, no doubt about it. Now in the Middle Ages men believed that in matters of reproduction thc woman was merely the vessel, the man's seed was what made the child. From that we've come full circle, we've come to the nearly total supremacy of women and men like you and me are reduced to—mere temporary agents.'

Teddy said to Anne that night, 'You don't think he's maybe a bit mad, do you? I mean broken down under the strain?'

'He hasn't got any strain here.'

'I'll tell you the other thing I was wondering. Linda's not up to anything, is she? I mean giving some other chap a whirl? Only she's all dressed up these days and she's lost weight. She looks years younger. If she's got someone that would account for poor old Michael, wouldn't it?'

It was their turn to go out in the evening and they were on their way back from the Krini Restaurant, the last one on the island to remain open after the middle of October. The night was starry, the moon three-quarters of a glowing white orb.

'There has to be a reason for him being like that. It's not normal. I don't spend my time worrying you're going to leave me and take the kids.'

'Is that what it is? He's afraid Linda's going to leave him?'

'It must be. He can't be getting in a tizzy over George Wilton's and Somebody Frost's problems.' Sage Teddy nodded his head. 'Human nature isn't like that,' he said. 'Let's go up to the fort, darling. We've never been up there by moonlight.'

They climbed to the top of the hill, Teddy puffing a bit on account of having had rather too much ouzo at the Krini. In summer the summit was floodlit but when the hotels closed the lights also went out. The moonlight was nearly as bright and the turf shone silver between the black shadows made by the broken walls. The Stamniots were desperate for rain now the tourist season was over, for the final boost to swell the olive crop. Teddy went up the one surviving flight of steps into the remains of the one surviving tower. He paused, waiting for Anne. He looked down but he couldn't see her.

'The Aegean's not always calm,' came her voice. 'Down here there's a current tears in and out like a mill race.'

He still couldn't see her, peering out from his look-out post. Then he did—just. She was silhouetted against the purplish starriness.

'Come back!' he shouted. 'You're too near the edge!'

He had made her jump. She turned quickly and at once slipped on the turf, going into a long slide on her back, legs in the air. Teddy ran down the steps. He ran across the turf, nearly falling himself, picked her up and hugged her.

'Suppose you'd fallen the other way?'

The palms of her hands were pitted with grit, in places the skin broken, where she had ineffectually made a grab at the sides of the fissure in the wall. 'I wouldn't have fallen at all if you hadn't shouted at me.'

At home the children were all asleep, Linda in bed but Michael still up. There were two empty wine bottles on the table and three glasses. A man they had met the night before in Agamemnon's had come in to have a drink with them, Michael said. He was German, from Heidelberg, here on his own for a late holiday.

'He was telling us about his divorce. His wife found a younger man with better job prospects who was able to offer Werner's children a swimming pool and riding lessons. Werner tried to kill himself but someone found him in time.'

What a gloomy way to spend an evening, thought Teddy, and was trying to find something cheerful to say when a shrill yell came from the children's room. Teddy couldn't for the life of him have said which one it was but Michael could. He knew his Alison's voice and in he went to comfort her. Teddy made a face at Anne and Anne cast up her eyes. Linda came out of her bedroom in her dressing gown.

'That awful man!' she said. 'Has he gone? He looks like a toad. Why don't we seem to know anyone any more who hasn't got a broken marriage?'

'You know us,' said Teddy.

'Yes, thank God.'

Michael took his children down to the beach most mornings. Teddy took his children to the beach too and would have gone to the bay on the other side of the headland except that Emma and Tim wanted to be with their cousins and Tim started bawling when Teddy demurred. So Teddy had to put up a show of being very pleased and delighted at the sight of Michael. The children were in and out of the pale clear green water. It was still very hot at noon.

'Like August,' said Teddy. 'By golly, it's a scorcher here in August.'

'Heat and cold don't mean all that much to me,' said Michael.

Resisting the temptation to say Bully for you or I should be so lucky or something on those lines, Teddy began to talk of plans for the following day, the hire car to Likythos, the visit to the monastery with the Byzantine relics and to the temple of Apollo. Michael turned on him a face so wretched, so hag-ridden, the eyes positively screwed up with pain, that Teddy who had been disliking and resenting him with schoolboy indignation was moved by pity to the depths of himself. The poor old boy, he thought, the poor devil. What's wrong with him?

'When Andrew and Alison are with me like they are now,' Michael began in a low rapid voice, 'it's not so bad. I always have that feeling, you see, that I could pick them up and run away with them and hide them.' He looked earnestly at Teddy. 'I'm strong, I'm young still. I could easily carry them both long distances. I could hide them. But there isn't anywhere in the civilized world you can hide for long, is there? Still, as I say, it's not so bad when they're with me, when there are just the three of us on our own. It's when I have to go out and leave them with *her*. I can't tell you how I feel going home. All the way in the train and walking up from the station I'm imagining going into that house and not hearing them, just silence and a note on the mantelpiece. I dread going home, I don't mind telling you, Teddy, and yet I long for it. Of course I do. I long to see them and know they're there and still mine. I say to myself, that's another day's reprieve. Sometimes I phone home half a dozen times in the day just to know she hasn't taken them away.'

Teddy was aghast. He didn't know what to say. It was as if the sun had gone in and all was cold and comfortless and hateful. The sea glittered, it looked hard and huge, an enemy.

'It hasn't been so bad while we've been here,' said Michael. 'Oh, I expect I've been a bore for you. I'm sorry about that, Teddy, I know what a misery I am. I keep thinking that when we get home it will all start again.'

'Has Linda then . . . ?' Teddy stammered. 'I mean, Linda isn't . . . ?'

Michael shook his head. 'Not yet, not yet. But she's young too, isn't she? She's attractive. She's got years yet ahead of her—years of torture for me, Teddy, before my kids grow up.'

Anne told Teddy she had spoken to Linda about it. 'She never looks at another man, she wouldn't. She's breaking her heart over Michael. Shc lost weight and bought those clothes because she felt she'd let herself go after Alison was born and she ought to try and be more attractive for him. This obsession of his is wearing her out. She wants him to see a psychiatrist but he won't.'

'The trouble is,' said Teddy, 'there's a certain amount of truth behind it. There's method in his madness. If Linda met a man she liked and went off with him—I mean, Michael could drive her to it if he went on like this—she *would* take the children and Michael *would* lose them.'

'Not you too!'

'Well, no, because I'm not potty like poor old Michael. I hope I'm a reasonable man. But it does make you think. A woman decides her marriage doesn't work any more and the husband can lose his kids, his home and maybe half his income. I mean if I were twenty-five again and hadn't ever met you I might think twice about getting married, by golly, I might.'

Their last evening it was Anne and Teddy's turn to baby-sit for Michael and Linda. They were dining with Werner at the Hotel Daphne. Linda wore a green silk dress, the colour of shallow sea water.

'More cosy chat about adultery and suicide, I expect,' said Teddy. Liking to have things pleasant about him, he settled himself with a large ouzo on the terrace under the vine. 'I shan't be altogether sorry to get home. And I'll tell you what. We could come at Easter next year, in Emma's school hols.'

'On our own,' said Anne.

Michael came in about ten. He was alone. Teddy saw that the palms of his hands were pitted as if he had held on to the rough surface of something stony. Anne got up.

'Where's Linda?'

He hesitated before replying. A look of cunning of the kind sane people's expressions never show spread over his face. His eyes shifted along the terrace, to the right, to the left. Then he looked at the palm of his right hand and began rubbing it with his thumb.

'At the hotel,' he said. 'With Werner.'

Anne cottoned on before he did, Teddy could see. She took a step towards Michael.

'What on earth do you mean, with Werner?'

'She's left me. She's going home to Germany with him tomorrow.'

'Michael, that just isn't true. She can't stand him, she told me so. She said he was like a toad.'

'Yes, she did,' said Teddy. 'I heard her say that.'

'All right, so she isn't with Werner. Have it your own way. Did the children wake up?'

'Never mind the children, Michael, they're OK. Tell us where Linda is, please. Don't play games.'

He didn't answer. He went back into the house, the bead curtain making a rattling swish as he passed through it. Anne and Teddy looked at each other.

'I'm frightened,' Anne said.

'Yes, so am I, frankly,' said Teddy.

The curtain rattled as Michael came through, carrying his children, Andrew over his shoulder, Alison in the crook of his arm, both of them more or less asleep.

'I scraped my hands on the stones up there,' he said. 'The turf's slippery as glass.' He gave Anne and Teddy a great wide empty smile. 'Just wanted to make sure the children were all right, I'll put them back to bed again.' He began to giggle with a kind of triumphant relief. 'I shan't lose them now. She won't take them from me now.'

THE GREEN ROAD TO QUEPHANDA

There used to be, not long ago, a London suburban line railway running up from Finsbury Park to Highgate, and further than that for all I know. They closed it down before I went to live at Highgate and at some point they took up the sleepers and the rails. But the track remains and a very strange and interesting track it is. There are people living in the vicinity of the old line who say they can still hear, at night and when the wind is right, the sound of a train pulling up the slope to Highgate and, before it comes into the old disused station, giving its long, melancholy, hooting call. A ghost train, presumably, on rails that have long been lifted and removed.

But this is not a ghost story. Who could conceive of the ghost, not of a person but of a place, and that place having no existence in the natural world? Who could suppose anything of a supernatural or paranormal kind happening to a man like myself, who am quite unimaginative and not observant at all?

An observant person, for instance, could hardly have lived for three years only two minutes from the old station without knowing of the existence of the line. Day after day, on my way to the Underground, I passed it, glanced down unseeing at the weed-grown platforms, the broken canopies. Where did I suppose those trees were growing, rowans and Spanish chestnuts and limes that drop their sticky black juice, like tar, that waved their branches in a long avenue high up in the air? What did I imagine that occasionally glimpsed valley was, lying between suburban back gardens? You may enter or leave the line at the bridges where there are always places for scrambling up or down, and at some actual steps, much overgrown, and gates or at least gateposts. I had been walking under or over these bridges (according as the streets where I walked passed under or over them) without ever asking myself what those bridges carried or crossed. It never even, I am sorry to say, occurred to me that there were rather a lot of bridges for a part of London where the only railway line, the Underground, ran deep in the bowels of the earth. I didn't think about them. As I walked under one of the brown brick tunnels I didn't look up to question its presence or ever once glance over a parapet. It was Arthur Kestrell who told me about the line, one evening while I was in his house.

* * *

Arthur was a novelist. I write 'was', not because he has abandoned his profession for some other, but because he is dead. I am not even sure whether one would call his books novels. They truly belong in that curious category, a fairly popular *genre*, that is an amalgam of science fiction, fairy tale and horror fantasy.

But Arthur, who used the pseudonym Blaise Fastnet, was no Mervyn Peake and no Lovecraft either. Not that I had read any of his books at the time of which I am writing. But Elizabeth, my wife, had. Arthur used sometimes to give us one of them on publication, duly inscribed and handed to us, presented indeed, with the air of something very precious and uniquely desirable being bestowed.

I couldn't bring myself to read them. The titles alone were enough to repel me: *Kallinarth, the Cloudling*, *The Quest of Kallinarth*, *Lord of Quephanda*, *The Grail-Seeker's Guerdon* and so forth. But I used somehow, without actually lying, to give Arthur the impression that I had read his latest, or I think I did. Perhaps, in fact, he saw through this, for he never enquired if I had enjoyed it or had any criticisms to make. Liz said they were 'fun', and sometimes—with kindly intent, I know—would refer to an incident or portion of dialogue in one of the books in Arthur's presence. 'As Kallinarth might have said,' she would say, or 'Weren't those the flowers Kallinarth picked for Valaquen when she woke from her long sleep?' This sort of thing only had the effect of making poor Arthur blush and look embarrassed. I believe that Arthur Kestrell was convinced in his heart that he was writing great literature, never perhaps to be recognized as such in his lifetime but for the appreciation of posterity. Liz, privately to me, used to call him the poor man's Tolkien.

He suffered from periods of black and profound depression. When these came upon him he couldn't write or read or even bring himself to go out on those marathon walks ranging across north London which he dearly loved when he was well. He would shut himself up in his Gothic house in that district where Highgate and Crouch End merge, and there he would hide and suffer and pace the floors, not answering the door, still less the telephone until, after five or six days or more, the mood of wretched despair had passed.

His books were never reviewed in the press. How it comes about that some authors' work never receives the attention of the critics is a mystery, but the implication, of course, is that it is beneath their notice. This ignoring of a new publication, this bland passing over with neither a smile nor a sneer, implies that the author's work is a mere commercially motivated repetition of his last book, a slight variation on a tried and lucrative theme, another stereotyped bubbler in a long line of profitable pot-boilers. Arthur, I believe, took it hard. Not that he told me so. But soon after Liz had scanned the papers for even a solitary line to announce a new Fastnet publication, one of these depressions of his would settle on him and he would go into hiding behind his grey, crenellated walls.

Emerging, he possessed for a while a kind of slow cheerfulness combined with a dogged attitude to life. It was always a pleasure to be with him, if for nothing else than the experience of his powerful and strange imagination whose vividness coloured those books of his, and in conversation gave an exotic slant to the observations he made and the opinions he uttered.

London, he always insisted, was a curious, glamorous and sinister city, hung on slopes and valleys in the north of the world. Did I not understand the charm it held for foreigners who thought of it with wistfulness as a grey Eldorado? I who had been born in it couldn't see its wonders, its contrasts, its wickednesses. In summer Arthur got me to walk with him to Marx's tomb, to the house where Housman wrote *A Shropshire Lad*, to the pond in the Vale of Health where Shelley sailed boats. We walked the Heath and we walked the urban woodlands and then one day, when I complained that there was nowhere left to go, Arthur told me about the track where the railway line had used to be. A long green lane, he said, like a country lane, four and a half miles of it, and smiling in his cautious way, he told me where it went. Over Northwood Road, over Stanhope Road, under Crouch End Hill, over Vicarage Road, under Crouch Hill, under Mount View, over Mount Pleasant Villas, over Stapleton Hall, under Upper Tollington Park, over Oxford Road, under Stroud Green Road, and so to the station at Finsbury Park.

'How do you get on to it?' I said.

'At any of the bridges. Or at Holmesdale Road. You can get on to it from the end of my garden.'

'Right,' I said. 'Let's go. It's a lovely day.'

'There'll be crowds of people on a Saturday,' said Arthur. 'The sun will be bright like fire and there'll be hordes of wild people and their bounding dogs and their children with music machines and tinned drinks.' This was the way Arthur talked, the words juicily or dreamily enunciated. 'You want to go up there when it's quiet, at twilight, at dusk, when the air is lilac and you can smell the bitter scent of the tansy.'

'Tomorrow night then. I'll bring Liz and we'll call for you and you can take us up there.'

But on the following night when we called at Arthur's house and stood under the stone archway of the porch and rang his bell, there was no answer. I stepped back and looked up at the narrow latticed windows, shaped like inverted shields. This was something which, in these circumstances, I had never done before.

Arthur's face looked back at me, blurred and made vague by the dark, diamond-paned glass, but unmistakeably his small wizened face, pale and with its short, sparse beard. It is a disconcerting thing to be looked at like this by a dear friend who returns your smile and your mouthed greeting with a dead, blank and unrecognizing stare. I suppose I knew then that poor Arthur wasn't quite sane any more. Certainly Liz and I both knew that he had entered one of his depressions and that it was useless to expect him to let us in.

We went off home, abandoning the idea of an exploration of the track that evening. But on the following day, work being rather slack at that time of the year, I found myself leaving the office and getting out of the tube train at Highgate at half-past four. Liz, I knew, would be out. On an impulse, I crossed the street and turned into Holmesdale Road. Many a time, walking there before, I had noticed what seemed an unexpectedly rural meadow lying to the north of the street, a meadow overshadowed by broad trees, though no more than fifty yards from the roar and stench of the Archway Road. Now I understood what it was. I walked down the slope, turned south-eastwards where the meadow narrowed and came on to a grassy lane.

It was about the width of an English country lane and it was bordered by hedges of buddleia on which peacock and small tortoiseshell butterflies basked. And I might have felt myself truly in the country had it not been for the backs of houses glimpsed all the time between the long leaves and the purple spires of the buddleia bushes. Arthur's lilac hour had not yet come. It was windless sunshine up on the broad green track, the clear, white light of a sun many hours yet from setting. But there was a wonderful warm and rural, or perhaps I should say pastoral, atmosphere about the place. I need Arthur's gift for words and Arthur's imagination to describe it properly and that I don't have. I can only say that there seemed, up there, to be a suspension of time and also of the hurrying, frenzied bustle, the rage to live, that I had just climbed up out of.

I went over the bridge at Northwood Road and over the bridge at Stanhope Road, feeling ashamed of myself for having so often walked unquestioningly *under* them. Soon the line began to descend, to become a valley rather than a causeway, with embankments on either side on which grew small, delicate birch trees and the rosebay willow herb and the giant hogweed. But there were no tansy flowers, as far as I could see. These are bright yellow double daisies borne in clusters on long stems and they have the same sort of smell as chrysanthemums. For all I know, they may be a sort of chrysanthemum or belonging to that family. Anyway, I couldn't see any or any lilac, but perhaps Arthur hadn't meant that and in any case it wouldn't be in bloom in July. I went as far as Crouch End Hill that first time and then I walked home by road. If I've given the impression there were no people on the line, this wasn't so. I passed a couple of women walking a labrador, two boys with bikes and a little girl in school uniform eating a choc ice.

Liz was intrigued to hear where I had been but rather cross that I hadn't waited until she could come too. So that evening, after we had had our meal, we walked along the line the way and the distance I had been earlier and the next night we ventured into the longer section. A tunnel blocked up with barbed wire prevented us from getting quite to the end but we covered nearly all of it and told each other we very likely hadn't missed much by this defeat.

The pastoral atmosphere disappeared after Crouch End Hill. Here there was an old station, the platforms alone still remaining, and under the bridge someone had dumped an old feather mattress—or plucked a dozen geese. The line became a rubbish dump for a hundred yards or so and then widened out into children's playgrounds with murals—and graffiti—on the old brick walls.

Liz looked back at the green valley behind. 'What you gain on the swings,' she said, 'you lose on the roundabouts.' A child in a rope seat swung past us, shrieking, nearly knocking us over.

All the prettiness and the atmosphere I have tried to describe was in that first section, Highgate station to Crouch End Hill. The next time I saw Arthur, when he was back in the world again, I told him we had explored the whole length of the line. He became quite excited.

'Have you now? All of it? It's beautiful, isn't it? Did you see the foxgloves? There must be a mile of foxgloves up there. And the mimosa? You wouldn't suppose mimosa could stand an English winter and I don't know of anywhere else it grows, but it flourishes up there. It's sheltered, you see, sheltered from all the frost and the harsh winds.'

Arthur spoke wistfully as if the frost and harsh winds he referred to were more metaphorical than actual, the coldness of life and fate and time rather than of climate. I didn't argue with him about the mimosa, though I had no doubt at all that he was mistaken. The line up there was exposed, not sheltered, and even if it had been, even if it had been in Cornwall or the warm Scilly Isles, it would still have been too cold for mimosa to survive. Foxgloves were another matter, though I hadn't seen any, only the hogweed with its bracts of dirty white flowers, garlic mustard and marestail, burdock and rosebay, and the pale leathery leaves of the coltsfoot. As the track grew rural again, past

Mount View, hawthorn bushes, not mimosa, grew on the embankment slopes.

'It belongs to Haringey Council.' Arthur's voice was always vibrant with expression and now it had become a drawl of scorn and contempt. 'They want to build houses on it. They want to plaster it with a great red sprawl of council houses, a disfiguring red naevus.' Poor Arthur's writing may not have been the effusion of genius he seemed to believe, but he certainly had a gift for the spoken word.

That August his annual novel was due to appear. Liz had been given an advance copy and had duly read it. Very much the same old thing, she said to me: Kallinarth, the hero-king in his realm composed of cloud; Valaquen, the maiden who sleeps, existing only in a dream-life, until all evil has gone out of the world; Xadatel and Finrael, wizard and warrior, heavenly twins. The title this time was *The Fountains of Zond*.

Arthur came to dinner with us soon after Liz had read it, we had three other guests, and while we were having our coffee and brandy I happened to say that I was sorry not to have any Drambuie as I knew he was particularly fond of it.

Liz said, 'We ought to have Xadatel here, Arthur, to magic you some out of the fountains of Zond.'

It was a harmless, even rather sympathetic, remark. It showed she knew Arthur's work and was conversant with the properties of these miraculous fountains which apparently produced nectar, fabulous elixirs or whatever was desired at a word from the wizard. Arthur, however, flushed and looked deeply offended. And afterwards, in the light of what happened, Liz endlessly reproached herself for what she had said.

'How were you to know?' I asked.

'I should have known. I should have understood how serious and intense he was about his work. The fountains produced—well, holy waters, you see, and I talked about it making Drambuie... Oh, I know it's absurd, but he *was* absurd, what he wrote meant everything to him. The same passion and inspiration—and muse, if you like, affected Shakespeare and Arthur Kestrell, it's just the end product that's different.'

Arthur, when she had made that remark, had said very stiffly, 'I'm afraid you're not very sensitive to imaginative literature, Elizabeth,' and he left the party early. Liz and I were both rather cross at the time and Liz said she was sure Tolkien wouldn't have minded if someone had made a gentle joke to him about Frodo.

A week or so after this there was a story in the evening paper to the effect that the Minister for the Environment had finally decided to forbid Haringey's plans for putting council housing on the old railway line. The Parkland Walk, as the newspaper called it. Four and a half miles of a disused branch of the London and North-Eastern Railway, was the way it was described, from Finsbury Park to Highgate and at one time serving Alexandra Palace. It was to remain in perpetuity a walking place. The paper mentioned wild life inhabiting the environs of the line, including foxes. Liz and I said we would go up there one evening in the autumn and see if we could see a fox. We never did go, I had reasons for not going near the place, but when we planned it I didn't know I had things to fear.

This was August, the end of August. The weather, with its English vagaries, had suddenly become very cold, more like November with north winds blowing, but in the last days of the month the warmth and the blue skies came back. We had received a formal thank-you note for that dinner from Arthur, a few chilly lines written for politeness' sake, but since then neither sight nor sound of him.

The Fountains of Zond had been published and, as was always the case with Arthur's, or Blaise Fastnet's, books, had been ignored by the critics. I supposed that one of his depressions would have set in, but nevertheless I thought I should attempt to see him and patch up this breach between us. On 1 September, a Saturday, I set off in the afternoon to walk along the old railway line to his house.

I phoned first, but there was no answer. It was a beautiful afternoon and Arthur might well have been sitting in his garden where he couldn't hear the phone. It was the first time I had ever walked to his house by this route, though it was shorter and more direct than by road, and the first time I had been up on the Parkland Walk on a Saturday. I soon saw what he had meant about the crowds who used it at the weekends. There were teenagers with transistors, giggling schoolgirls, gangs of slouching youths, mobs of children, courting couples, middle-aged picnickers. At Northwood Road boys and girls were leaning against the parapet of the bridge, some with guitars, one with a drum, making enough noise for a hundred.

I remember that as I walked along, unable because of the noise and the press of people to appreciate nature or the view, that I turned my thoughts concentratedly on Arthur Kestrell. And I realized quite suddenly that although I thought of him as a close friend and liked him and enjoyed his company, I had never even tried to enter into his feelings or to understand him. If I had not actually laughed at his books, I had treated them in a light-hearted cavalier way, almost with contempt. I hadn't bothered to read a single one of them, a single page of one of them. And it seemed to me, as I strolled along that grassy path towards the Stanhope Road bridge, that it must be a terrible thing to pour all your life and soul and energy and passion into works that are remaindered in the bookshops, ignored by the critics, dismissed by paperback publishers, and taken off library shelves only by those who are attracted by the jackets and are seeking escape.

I resolved there and then to read every one of Arthur's books that we had. I made a kind of vow to myself to show an interest in them to Arthur, to make him discuss them with me. And so fired was I by this resolve that I determined to start at once, the moment I saw Arthur. I would begin by apologizing for Liz and then I would tell him (without revealing, of course, that I had so far read nothing of his) that I intended to make my way carefully through all his books, treating them as an *oeuvre*, beginning with *Kallinarth, the Cloudling* and progressing through all fifteen or however many it was up to *The Fountains of Zond*. He might treat this with sarcasm, I thought, but he wouldn't keep that up when he saw I was sincere. My enthusiasm might do him positive good, it might help cure those terrible depressions which lately had seemed to come more frequently.

Arthur's house stood on this side, the Highgate side, of Crouch End Hill. You couldn't see it from the line, though you could get on to the line from it. This was because the line had by then entered its valley out of which you had to climb into Crescent Road before the Crouch End Hill bridge. I climbed up and walked back and rang Arthur's bell but got no answer. So I looked up at those Gothic lattices as I had done on the day Liz was with me and though I didn't see Arthur's face this time, I was sure I saw a curtain move. I called up to him, something I had never done before, but I had never felt it mattered before, I had never previously had this sense of urgency and importance in connection with Arthur.

'Let me in, Arthur,' I called to him. 'I want to see you. Don't hide yourself, there's a good chap. This is important.'

There was no sound, no further twitch of curtain. I rang again and banged on the door. The house seemed still and wary, waiting for me to go away.

'All right,' I said through the letterbox. 'Be like that. But I'm coming back. I'll go for a bit of a walk and then I'll come back and I'll expect you to let me in.'

I went back down on to the line, meeting the musicians from Northwood bridge who were marching in the Finsbury Park direction, banging their drum and joined now by two West Indian boys with zithers. A child had been stung by a bee that was on one of the buddleias and an alsatian and a yellow labrador were fighting under the bridge. I began to walk quickly towards Stanhope Road, deciding to ring Arthur as soon as I got home, to keep on ringing until he answered.

Why was I suddenly so determined to see him, to break in on him, to make him know that I understood? I don't know why and I suppose I never will know, but this was all part of it, having some definite connection, I think, with what happened. It was as if, for those moments, perhaps half an hour all told, I became intertwined with Arthur Kestrell, part of his mind almost or he part of mine. He was briefly and for that one time the most important person in my world.

I never saw him again. I didn't go back. Some few yards before the Stanhope bridge, where the line rose once more above the streets, I felt an impulse to look back and see if from there I could see his garden or even see him in his garden. But the hawthorn, small birches, the endless buddleia grew thick here and higher far than a man's height. I crossed to the right hand, or northern, side and pushed aside with my arms the long purple flowers and rough dark leaves, sending up into the air a cloud of black and orange butterflies.

Instead of the gardens and backs of houses which I expected to see, there stretched before me, long and straight and raised like a causeway, a green road turning northwards out of the old line. This debouching occurred, in fact, at my feet. Inadvertently, I had parted the bushes at the very point where a secondary branch left the line, the junction now overgrown with weeds and wild shrubs.

I stood staring at it in wonder. How could it be that I had never noticed it before, that Arthur hadn't mentioned it? Then I remembered that the newspaper story had said something about the line 'serving Alexandra Palace'. I had assumed this meant the line had gone on to Alexandra Palace after Highgate, but perhaps not, definitely not, for here was a branch line, leading northwards, leading straight towards the palace and the park.

I hadn't noticed it, of course, because of the thick barrier of foliage. In winter, when the leaves were gone, it would be apparent for all to see. I decided to walk along it, check that it actually led where I thought it would, and catch a bus from Alexandra Palace home.

The grass underfoot was greener and far less worn than on the main line. This seemed to indicate that fewer people came along here, and I was suddenly aware that I had left the crowds behind. There was no one to be seen, not even in the far distance.

Which was not, in fact, so very far. I was soon wondering how I had got the impression when I first parted those bushes that the branch line was straight and treeless. For tall trees grew on either side of the path, oaks and beeches such as were never seen on the other line, and ahead of me their branches met overhead and their fine frondy twigs interlaced. Around their trunks I at last saw the foxgloves and the tansy Arthur had spoken of, and the further I went the more the air seemed perfumed with the scent of wild flowers.

The green road—I found myself spontaneously and unaccountably calling this branch line the green road—began to take on the aspect of a grove or avenue and to widen. It was growing late in the afternoon and a mist was settling over London as often happens after a warm day in late summer or early autumn. The slate roofs, lying a little beneath me, gleamed dully silver through this sleepy, gold-shot mist. Perhaps, I thought, I should have the good luck to see a fox. But I saw nothing, no living thing, not a soul passed me or overtook me, and when I looked back I could see only the smooth grassy causeway stretching back and back, deserted, still, serene and pastoral, with the mist lying in fine streaks beneath and beside it. No birds sang and no breeze ruffled the feather-light, golden, downy, sweet-scented tufts of the mimosa flowers. For, yes, there was mimosa here. I paused and looked at it and marvelled.

It grew on either side of the path as vigorously and luxuriantly as it grows by the Mediterranean, the gentle swaying wattle. Its perfume filled the air, and the perfume of the humbler foxglove and tansy was lost. Did the oaks shelter it from the worst of the frost? Was there by chance some warm spring that flowed under the earth here, in this part of north London where there are many patches of woodland and many green spaces? I picked a tuft of mimosa to take home to Liz, to prove I'd been here and seen it.

I walked for a very long way, it seemed to me, before I finally came into Alexandra Park. I hardly know this park, and apart from passing its gates by car my only experience of it till then had been a visit some years before to take Liz to an exhibition of paintings in the palace. The point in the grounds to which my green road had brought me was somewhere I had never seen before. Nor had I ever previously been aware of this aspect of Alexandra Palace, under whose walls almost the road led. It was more like Versailles than a Victorian greenhouse (which is how I had always thought of the palace) and in the oblong lakes which flanked the flight of steps before me were playing surely a hundred fountains. I looked up this flight of steps and saw pillars and arches, a soaring elevation of towers. It was to here then, I thought, right up under the very walls, that the trains had come. People had used the line to come here for shows, for exhibitions, for concerts. I stepped off on to the stone stairs, descended a dozen of them to ground level and looked out over the park.

London was invisible, swallowed now by the white mist which lay over it like cirrus. The effect was curious, something I had never seen before while standing on solid ground. It was the view you get from an aircraft when it has passed above the clouds and you look down on to the ruffled tops of them. I began to walk down over wide green lawns. Still there were no people, but I had guessed it likely that they locked the gates on pedestrians after a certain hour.

However, when I reached the foot of the hill the iron gates between their Ionic columns were still open. I came out into a street I had never been in before, in a district I didn't know, and there found a taxi which took me home. On the journey I remember thinking to myself that I would ask Arthur about this curious terminus to the branch line and get him to tell me something of the history of all that grandeur of lawns and pillars and ornamental water.

* * *

I was never to have the opportunity of asking him anything. Arthur's cleaner, letting herself into the Gothic house on Monday morning, found him hanging from one of the beams in his writing room. He had been dead, it was thought, since some time on Saturday afternoon. There was a suicide note, written in

Arthur's precise hand and in Arthur's wordy, pedantic fashion: 'Bitter disappointment at my continual failure to reach a sensitive audience or to attract understanding of my writing has led me to put an end to my life. There is no one who will suffer undue distress at my death. Existence has become insupportable and I cannot contemplate further sequences of despair.'

Elizabeth told me that in her opinion it was the only rcvicw shc had cvcr known him to have which provoked poor Arthur to kill himself. She had found it in the paper herself on that Saturday afternoon while I was out and had read it with a sick feeling of dread for how Arthur would react. The critic, with perhaps nothing else at that moment to get his teeth into, had torn *The Fountains of Zond* apart and spat out the shreds.

He began by admitting he would not normally have wasted his typewriter ribbon (as he put it) on sci-fi fantasy trash, but he felt the time had come to campaign against the flooding of the fiction market with such stuff. Especially was it necessary in a case like this where a flavour of epic grandeur was given to the action, where there was much so-called 'fine writing' and where heroic motives were attributed to stereotyped or vulgar characters, so that innocent or young readers might be misled into believing that this was 'good' or 'valuable' literature. There was a lot more in the same vein. With exquisite cruelty the reviewer had taken character after character and dissected each, holding the exposed parts up to stinging ridicule. If Arthur had read it, and it seemed likely that he had, it was no wonder he had felt he couldn't bear another hour of existence.

All this deflected my thoughts, of course, away from the green road. I had told Liz about it before we heard of Arthur's death and we had intended to go up there together, yet somehow, after that dreadful discovery in the writing room of the Gothic house, we couldn't bring ourselves to walk so close by his garden or to visit those places where he would have loved to take us. I kept wondering if I had really seen that curtain move when I had knocked at his door or if it had only been a flicker of the sunlight. Had he already been dead by then? Or had he perhaps been contemplating what he was about to do? Just as Liz reproached herself for that remark about the fountains, so I reproached myself for walking away, for not hammering on that door, breaking a window, getting in by some means. Yet, as I said to her, how could anyone have known?

In October I did go up on to the old railway line. Someone we knew living in Milton Park wanted to borrow my electric drill, and I walked over there with it, going down from the Stanhope Road bridge on the southern side. Peter offered to drive me back but it was a warm afternoon, the sun on the point of setting, and I had a fancy to look at the branch line once more, I climbed up on the bridge and turned eastwards.

For the most part the leaves were still on the bushes and trees, though turning red and gold. I calculated pretty well where the turn-off was and pushed my way through the buddleias. Or I thought I had calculated well, but when I stood on the ridge beyond the hedge all I could see were the gardens of Stanhope Road and Avenue Road. I had come to the wrong place, I thought, it must be further along. But not much further, for very soon what had been a causeway became a valley. My branch line hadn't turned out of that sort of terrain, I hadn't had to climb to reach it.

Had I made a mistake and had it been on the *other* side of the Stanhope Road bridge? I turned back, walking slowly, making sorties through the buddleias to look northwards, but I couldn't anywhere find that turn-off to the branch line. It seemed to me then that, whatever I thought I remembered, I must in fact have climbed up the embankment to reach it and the junction must be far nearer the bridge at Crouch End Hill than I had believed. By then it was getting dark. It was too dark to go back, I should have been able to see nothing.

'We'll find it next week,' I said to Liz.

She gave me a rather strange look. 'I didn't

say anything at the time,' she said, 'because we were both so upset over poor Arthur, but I was talking to someone in the Highgate Society and she said there never was a branch line. The line to Alexandra Palace went on beyond Highgate.'

'That's nonsense,' I said. 'I can assure you I walked along it. Don't you remember my telling you at the time?'

'Are you absolutely sure you couldn't have imagined it?'

'*Imagined it*? You know I haven't any imagination.'

Liz laughed. 'You're always saying that but I think you have. You're one of the most imaginative people I ever knew.'

I said impatiently, 'Be that as it may. I walked a good two miles along that line and came out in Alexandra Park, right under the palace, and walked down to Wood Green or Muswell Hill or somewhere and got a cab home. Are you and your Highgate Society friends saying I imagined oak trees and beech trees and mimosa? Look, that'll prove it, I picked a piece of mimosa, I picked it and put it in the pocket of my green jacket.'

'Your green jacket went to the cleaners last month.'

I wasn't prepared to accept that I had imagined or dreamed the green road. But the fact remains that I was never able to find it. Once the leaves were off the trees there was no question of delving about under bushes to hunt for it. The whole northern side of the old railway line lay exposed to the view and the elements and much of its charm was lost. It became what it really always was, nothing more or less than a ridge, a long strip of waste ground running across north London, over Northwood Road, over Stanhope Road, under Crouch End Hill, over Vicarage Road, under Crouch Hill, under Mount View, over Mount Pleasant Villas, over Stapleton Hall, under Upper Tollington Park, over Oxford Road, under Stroud Green Road, and so to the station at Finsbury Park. And nowhere along its length, for I explored every inch, was there a branch line running north to Alexandra Palace.

'You imagined it,' said Liz, 'and the shock of Arthur dying like that made you think it was real.'

'But Arthur wasn't dead then,' I said 'or I didn't know he was.'

My invention, or whatever it was, of the branch line would have remained one of those mysteries which everyone, I suppose, has in his life, though I can't say I have any others in mine, had it not been for a rather curious and unnerving conversation which took place that winter between Liz and our friends from Milton Park. In spite of my resolutions made on that memorable Saturday afternoon, I had never brought myself to read any of Arthur's books.

What now would have been the point? He was no longer there for me to talk to about them. And there was another reason. I felt my memory of him might be spoiled if there was truth in what the critic had said and his novels were full of false heroics and sham fine writing. Better feel with whatever poet it was who wrote:

> I wept as I remembered how often thou and I
> Have tired the sun with talking and sent him
> down the sky.

Liz, however, had had her interest in *The Chronicles of Kallinarth* revived and had reread every book in the series, passing them on as she finished each to Peter and Jane. That winter afternoon in the living room at Milton Park the three of them were full of it, Kallinarth, cloud country, Valaquen, Xadatel, the lot, and it was they who tired the sun with talking and sent him down the sky. I sat silent, not really listening, not taking part at all, but thinking of Arthur whose house was not far from here and who would have marvelled to hear of this detailed knowledge of his work.

I don't know which word of theirs it was that caught me or what electrifying phrase jolted me out of my reverie so that I leaned forward, intent. Whatever it was, it had sent a little shiver through my body. In that warm room I felt suddenly cold.

'No, it's not in *Kallinarth, the Cloudling*,' Jane was saying. 'It's *The Quest of Kallinarth*. Kallinarth goes out hunting early in the morning and he meets Xadatel and Finrael coming on horseback up the green road to the palace.'

'But that's not the first mention of it. In the first book there's a long description of the avenue where the procession comes up for Kallinarth to be crowned at the fountains of Zond and . . .'

'It's in all the books surely,' interrupted Peter. 'It's his theme, his leitmotiv, that green road with the yellow wattle trees that leads up to the royal palace of Quephanda . . .'

'Are you all right, darling?' Liz said quickly. 'You've gone as white as a ghost.'

'White with boredom,' said Peter. 'It must be terrible for him us talking about this rubbish and he's never even read it.'

'Somehow I feel I know it without reading it,' I managed to say.

They changed the subject. I didn't take much part in that either, I couldn't. I could only think, it's fantastic, it's absurd, I couldn't have got into his mind or he into mine, that couldn't have happened at the point of his death. Yet what else?

And I kept repeating over and over to myself, he reached his audience, he reached his audience at last.